Love is
a time of enchantment:
in it all days are fair and all fields
green. Youth is blest by it,
old age made benign:
the eyes of love see
roses blooming in December,
and sunshine through rain. Verily
is the time of true-love
a time of enchantment — and
Oh! how eager is woman
to be bewitched!

HOLD BACK TOMORROW

Greta Lindstrom, a young teacher from Minnesota, could imagine no place more perfect than Gotland, Sweden's playground, for the marriage of her cousin Margrit and her handsome fiancé Erik. As Margrit finished her work, Erik guided Greta around the magnificent Swedish countryside. But as Greta spent more time with Erik, their friendship seemed to blossom into something else. Yet how could she allow herself to fall in love with the man her cousin was about to marry?

ANNE STARR

HOLD BACK TOMORROW

Complete and Unabridged

ULVERSCROFT
Leicester

First published in the
United States of America

First Large Print Edition
published December 1992

British Library CIP Data

Starr, Anne
    Hold back tomorrow.—Large print ed.—
Ulverscroft large print series: romance
I. Title
823 [F]

    ISBN 0–7089–2778–5

Published by
F. A. Thorpe (Publishing) Ltd.
Anstey, Leicestershire
Set by Words & Graphics Ltd.
Anstey, Leicestershire
Printed and bound in Great Britain by
T. J. Press (Padstow) Ltd., Padstow, Cornwall

1

"SUCH roses — oh, Margit!" Greta Lindstrom breathed deeply of the redolent Baltic air and gazed wonder-filled at masses of pink bursting from the roadside gardens flashing past her cousin's silver Ferrari.

"Instead of Sweden's Playground" — she smiled delightedly at Margit behind the wheel — "your island ought to be called Sweden's Gardenland."

Margit returned the smile, pleased that her American relative had found her homeland beautiful.

"I suppose it does seem like a big garden," she said. "Here in Gotland we take our roses too much for granted perhaps. It's good to be reminded of how lucky we are to have their blossoms everywhere."

"And to have their perfume to breathe instead of ordinary oxygen," Greta added with a laugh.

Once again she rested her gaze on her

blond cousin and was filled with renewed admiration for the glowing beauty of Margit, who was even more striking than her photographs had shown her to be. Corn-silk hair falling to her shoulders . . . those tender, pale eyes . . . and a complexion as creamy and smooth as the rose petals themselves. Yes, her lovely, impulsive cousin would make a stunning bride.

Greta herself was not as beautiful as Margit, but there was a calm, arresting quality in her deeper-hued eyes, and a steadfastness that her more exuberant cousin appeared to lack. Often Greta was reserved and shy, but deep within her a current of romantic idealism sometimes brought stars to her blue eyes and caused a compelling kind of vibrancy to radiate from her. She was taller than Margit, but otherwise the two cousins shared the same slender, graceful build. They were, in fact, Greta noted with a warming glow, very much like the sisters they had long considered themselves to be.

Greta spoke again, a tremor of excitement tingeing her soft voice. "I have to pinch myself to believe I'm really here at last."

"So do I," Margit answered. "Do you know, when your letter came accepting my invitation to be maid of honor in my wedding, I sat down and cried?"

"That's not very flattering," Greta said ruefully, but beneath her teasing tone, her heart swelled with happiness. It was wonderful to feel so at ease with Margit. Until an hour ago when the Stockholm ferry docked in Visby harbor, they had never met. But the two girls now twenty-four, had corresponded since they were children. For years Margit's letters in carefully written English had arrived every few months at the Minnesota farm where Greta grew up and Greta's faltering replies in Swedish had returned to Margit's Gotland farm with about the same frequency.

Their grandfathers had been brothers, and though thousands of miles had eventually separated them, the two branches of the family had remained close through three generations. Greta, however, was the first of the American branch to return to Gotland since her grandfather had set sail from its shores in his early twenties.

"The whole clan at home will be on pins and needles until I'm back with every detail of the wedding," she told Margit now, imagining with a shiver of delight the exciting moment when Margit became Mrs. Erik Lennart, wife of one of Sweden's most-talked-about young movie directors.

Margit cut abruptly through her thoughts. "Please don't talk of going back already. We plan to keep you with us at least until your school starts in the fall."

"As if you'll care where I am after you've said your vows." Greta's eyes danced. "Five minutes after the wedding you won't be thinking of anyone except yourself and Erik."

To her surprise, Margit answered sharply. "That isn't true. Family means everything to me."

"Oh, I didn't mean — Of course it does. To me, too." Swiftly Greta changed the subject. "Tell me about Erik. Your letters were so filled with details for making my trip easier that you hardly mentioned him at all."

Margit kept her eyes on the winding road, banked now as they came out into the open country with masses of wild blue chicory and pink tar blossoms. "He's a movie director — but you know that."

Greta nodded. "Me, along with half the rest of the world. Erik is quite a celebrity. Even in the backwoods of Minnesota everyone has seen *Seasons of Torment*."

Margit made a wry face. "Not my favorite of his pictures, I can tell you that."

"Oh?" Greta's brows lifted. "I found it very moving. And the reviews were wonderful."

"Erik hates it. It was his last picture, you know."

"You sound as if he's never going to make another."

"He may not. At the moment he's disillusioned with the movie business. He spends most of his time here in Gotland, licking his wounds at his farm."

"Licking his wounds!" Greta's lips parted. "But he's so successful — "

Margit shrugged. "He's made heaps

5

of money, of course. But that isn't enough. Not for Erik at least. He's sick of the whole business. All the fakery and conniving that's connected with it. The superficial actresses, the glitter and tinsel." She slid her pale eyes across to Greta. "You know how it is — coming from America."

For a moment Greta was startled. Then she realized that Margit's lighthearted mood had returned, and they laughed together.

"I certainly *don't* know," said Greta. "The world of a third-grade teacher extends no farther than the box office, I'm afraid."

Margit sobered again. "I envy you your career."

"Really?" Once more Greta was surprised. The remark seemed a strange one, coming from a girl who had everything to look forward to. Besides, Margit had a career of her own as a potter in a shop-studio shared with two other craftsmen.

Greta was about to make mention of that when it occurred to her that perhaps Erik Lennart was a man who expected his wife to devote herself entirely to him, and she kept silent, turning her attention instead to the clumps of white-barked birch lining the road Margit had turned onto.

"Are we nearing the farm?"

Margit nodded. "But we'll come to Erik's farm first. They're adjacent — his and ours."

Greta felt excitement crowding at her throat. "Will I meet him now?"

Everything about Margit and Margit's romance with Erik had the aura of a fairy tale about it. Illusion left over from childhood, Greta guessed, remembering how she had cherished that first letter from Margit when she was ten. The funny slanting words . . . the way the paper had smelled. Of the sea, she had thought then, and saved the stamp. She had it still.

"I've dreamed of him in a dozen ways," she confided in a rush.

"Of Erik?" Margit seemed amused. "Hasn't his fame at least allowed him a photograph in one of your newspapers?"

Greta's fair cheeks colored slightly. "I'm afraid I never thought to notice

— until you wrote that you were marrying him."

"Then tell me how you've pictured him," Margit said lightly. "What is he like?"

But a sudden embarrassment silenced Greta. She felt as if she were ten again — awkward and silly and foolishly romantic in contrast to Margit, who seemed so composed, so matter-of-fact for a bride. Greta reminded herself that the wedding was still a month away. And yet . . . Her heart skipped a beat. If it were I who were getting married . . .

Margit broke into her thoughts. "There's Erik now." Steering the Ferrari — her engagement gift from her fiancé — to the side of the road, she said in a voice tinged with a peculiar irony, "Gaze on the original and say good-bye to your dream-world illusions."

Eagerly Greta swung around. Shading her eyes with one hand, she saw outlined against the late-evening sky a man atop a roan horse riding toward them with an easy, careless grace, his head up, his hands loosely grasping the reins.

As if he owns the world, Greta thought,

and felt a stirring within her as her gaze moved over the man's powerful body. He was very much as she had envisioned him. Like a Viking, she thought in wonder. Then as he drew up to the hedgerow and dismounted, she caught her breath. But his hair was dark!

She had anticipated the wide shoulders, the narrow hips sheathed now in brown riding pants, the sense of power emanating from him . . . but Gotlanders were supposed to be fair!

For affirmation she swung back toward Margit's pale beauty only to behold the emptiness in her cousin's smile. Amazed, she saw no joy in Margit's expression and not the slightest trace of eagerness or delight.

Greta stared. Was that a look of love?

Then suddenly she was aware that Erik Lennart had approached the car. She looked around and a pair of dark, brooding eyes met hers. A shiver of excitement rippled up her spine as she felt the warmth radiating from the tanned arm touching hers on the rolled-down window's edge. Again the arresting power she had sensed as she watched him cross the meadow swept over her.

"Hello — "At once she wondered where she had found the breath for even that one word. Her cousin's fiancé was the most disturbingly attractive man she had ever seen.

There was a sensuous unevenness about his craggy features that lent an extra dimension to his rugged good looks. Heavy brows came together over a straight, aristocratic nose, but below that, his strong mouth appeared almost angry in its tantalizing stubbornness. His chin was square, but interestingly off-center, and in his eyes there was a look so penetrating that Greta shrank from it. Gratefully she heard Margit ending the awkward moment with an introduction.

For an instant afterward Erik continued to regard her solemnly. Then he said in a low-timbred voice startling in its resonance, "I'm glad you're here, Greta. Without the promise of your arrival, Margit might never have been able to settle on a wedding date."

Flattery? Greta smiled, but Margit spoke again before she could think of a reply.

"Greta has been dreaming of you, Erik."

Greta reddened, but Erik took the remark in stride.

"Really?" His dark-eyed look skimmed her flushed face before he returned his attention to Margit. "And you, my love," he challenged quietly. "What have you been dreaming of?"

"Our wedding, of course." Margit's delicate chin came up. "Greta and I were just speaking of it."

Listening, Greta had the dazed feeling that Margit and Erik were fencing. But of course, she thought, her eyes moving from one handsome, expressionless face to the other, this must be the way it was with sophisticated people who fell in love.

She had never considered Margit sophisticated before, but if a man as suavely assured as Erik Lennart had asked her to be his wife, evidently she must be.

Greta shifted uncomfortably and watched Erik and Margit exchange another unreadable look. Then simultaneously they became aware of her again.

"What do you think of our island?" Erik said at the same time Margit spoke.

"Mother and Father must be pacing the floor by now, wondering where we are, Greta."

Once more Greta started to speak, but Margit broke in again. "Will you come with us, Erik?"

"Not now." He moved back from the car, smoothing the flank of his horse with strong, capable-looking hands. "I'll ride over later. We have a new ram I'm eager to see."

"How exciting," Margit said lightly, but there was a biting edge in her voice. "Sorry, Greta. I hope you're not offended at having to play second fiddle to a sheep."

Unsmiling, Erik answered the taunt. "I'm sure Greta realizes that my interest in a new ram in no way diminishes the importance of her arrival."

"As if anything could do that." Margit tossed her blond mane and shifted the car into gear. Lifting her hand in a careless wave, she said over her shoulder. "We'll see you for supper, then. If you come early enough I may give you a drink and let you watch my sunset."

Still bemused by her cousin's flippant attitude, which contrasted sharply with the warmth and tenderness Margit had displayed when they met, Greta glanced back, watching as Erik remounted his horse.

After her first greeting she had not spoken a word to him, she mused regretfully. What a dummy he must think her! But even if Margit had given her a chance, she wasn't sure she could have thought of anything to say in response to those brooding brown eyes. Amazed to find that she was still a little breathless, she turned to Margit. "Your Erik is quite wonderful, isn't he?"

Margit answered cryptically. "A great many people think so."

There seemed no appropriate reply to that, and Greta berating herself for the disturbing sense of uneasiness that had suddenly clouded her day, confined the rest of her comments to the beauty of the countryside.

★ ★ ★

The Olsson farm lay on the green brown of a gentle rise about a mile beyond where Margit and Greta had met Erik. With their burnished sides and red-tiled roofs, the house and its barns were typical of a dozen others Greta had noticed on the drive from Visby, but even the softening light of late evening could not disguise the fact that the Olsson ancestral farm was slighty more rundown than the others she had seen. The shutters and steps were in need of a fresh coat of paint and a general atmosphere of disrepair seemed to hang over everything.

As if Margit were seeing her home anew through Greta's eyes, she offered a mild apology as she parked the Ferrari before the leaning front gate.

"Father was ill in the spring, you know. I'm afraid during his convalescence we let things go down a bit."

"It's a wonderfully cozy-looking farm," Greta answered enthusiastically — and meant it — but she could not help contrasting it to the trim appearance of Erik's property, nor could she help noticing a little sadly that the expensive car they were climbing out of made

14

everything that surrounded the Olsson place even more shabby than perhaps it really was.

Her somber mood did not last long, however, once they had gone inside. There everything was sparkling and shining. Crisp white curtains hung at the windows and a lived-in homeyness pervaded every room. The Nordic-style furniture was sturdy and gave forth the glowing patina of age. Wonderful smells hung in the air, and the meal Cousin Hannah was preparing in the spotless kitchen was as familiar to Greta as a thousand others her own mother had cooked through the years.

By suppertime as Greta gazed across the table at the kind faces of Margit's parents, her joy had returned full force, but even so she felt an occasional prick of homesickness and longing for her own parents to be a part of this precious first evening of getting acquainted.

Still, on the other hand, she felt she had known the Olssons always. For years she had shared her secrets with Margit, and now, looking at her cousin's mother and father, she felt close to them as well.

In the slant of Kenneth Olsson's forehead she saw her own mother's brow repeated, and listening to the grace he had offered before the meal, she had heard echoes of her father's ritual blessing. The two families lived an ocean apart and were separated by generations, but they shared the same Swedish heritage and the same blood, and Greta felt very much at home.

As for her feelings toward Erik, precious little remained of the strain meeting him had produced. When he had joined them at six for a strong Gotland beer called *dragol*, he had at once made himself comfortable in the homey sitting room that looked out across waving fields of grain toward the setting sun. There was no repetition of the tenseness that she believed now she had imagined between him and Margit, and she was gratified to see, as he took a seat next to her cousin on the couch, that his arm draped Margit's shoulder with accustomed ease and that they chatted amiably. Greta was further reassured in the dining room when she saw how fond Erik seemed of Kenneth and Hannah and how easily they all spoke

16

of the approaching wedding day.

If anything had been amiss earlier, Greta decided as she and Margit cleared the table, her own presence must have been responsible. She had to remember she was a stranger — if not to Margit, certainly to Erik. Naturally he had felt some constraint meeting her for the first time.

But everything was fine now, she thought with satisfaction as Erik took Margit's slender hand and started with her toward the sitting room.

"Come and join us," he said to Greta when he saw her watching, but she shook her head.

"I've been looking forward to a private chat with Hannah," she answered, smiling. "I hope to have it while we do the dishes."

Margit hesitated, frowning. "I'm the one who should be doing the dishes."

"Nonsense," said Greta briskly. "If you intend to treat me as a guest, then I'll catch the next ferry back to Stockholm."

"Join us later, then," Margit said.

Later, however, when the gleaming

white pottery that Margit had made for her mother was set again in neat rows on the cupboard shelves, Greta discovered that Erik was alone, standing with his back toward the sitting room, staring out through the windows at the summer night.

When he heard Greta's step he turned, and reading her puzzled expression, he said without a smile, "Margit is on the telephone."

Greta's heart lurched as she saw the return of the brooding look to his eyes. Wetting her lips, she offered an opening for conversation.

"Kenneth and Hannah have gone for a walk. In the woods, I believe they said."

His gaze traveled over her, and she noticed with relief the set look around his mouth relaxing a bit. "Their walk is an evening ritual with them. They have been married for thirty-two years, but they still take pleasure in their moments alone."

His answer made it easy for Greta to respond. "My parents are the same, but their privacy is limited, I'm afraid." A

18

fond smile lit her face. "I have four young brothers. Our home is always full of the noise and confusion of their friends coming and going."

His dark brows rose. "And your friends? What of them?"

"I no longer live at home. She felt her cheeks heat up. Why was he staring at her so?

"You are a teacher, Margit tells me."

"Yes, I teach third grade. I have an apartment in town near my school, but most weekends I spend at the farm."

His look sharpened, but he made no further comment, moving instead around to the couch where he motioned for her to sit down with him.

Greta hesitated. "I hope I'm not intruding."

"Intruding upon what?" His laugh was not unpleasant, but still it sent a peculiar shiver over Greta's bare arms. "I'm alone, as you can see," he went on, "and probably I shall be for some time. Margit can be rather voluble on the telephone. I shall be glad for your company." He set his head to one side and intensified his stare. "It's

19

quite astonishing, you know, to observe how closely you cousins resemble each other."

So that was the cause for his scrutiny! Greta flushed, relieved. "Do you think so?" She took her place beside him, being careful nonetheless to reserve the space of a cushion between them. She had lost most of the shyness she had felt earlier, but she still found Erik's rugged good looks unsettling.

"Margit and I are the same type, of course. Fair, Nordic — " She hesitated, aware again that the man beside her, though he was certainly Swedish, was neither fair nor Nordic-appearing.

The similarity goes beyond that," Erik said, picking up where she had left off. "There is an identical expression in your eyes." His own gaze narrowed. "A certain straightforwardness that is tremendously appealing. That was what first attracted me to Margit, in fact. That look of — " He paused. "I suppose one would call it purity."

Purity! Greta was flattered, but at the same time the remark made her feel too much like a milkmaid or a

Victorian spinster to think it entirely complimentary.

"Your director's eye is trained to watch for such things, I suppose," she murmured.

This time his laugh was husky, surprising somehow, and a bit overwhelming too. "Perhaps that's it." His gaze held steady. "Perhaps I am always typecasting, even here in Gotland."

"You aren't engaged in the movie business at the moment?" she ventured.

He gave her a sharp look as though he knew she was aware beforehand of his answer. "Not at the moment."

He shifted, and she saw the long line of his muscular thighs tighten beneath his close-fitting riding breeches and smelled again the scent of shaving lotion mixed with fresh air and sunshine that she had noticed going in to supper.

"Currently I am involved in breeding sheep, and I also breed *russ*, but more as a hobby than anything else."

"*Russ?*" Greta blinked.

"Miniature ponies. They've run wild on the island since the time of the Vikings. My goal is to strengthen through

21

controlled breeding the rare old qualities that have been gradually dying out because of their uninhibited moorland roamings."

"How fascinating!" It was plain from Greta's eager expression that her interest was genuine, and Erik, appreciating that it was, went on in more detail. As Greta listened she saw the brooding look that had veiled his eyes when she entered the room lifting and a sparkle of enthusiasm taking its place.

Eagerly she questioned him further. "*Russ* are like Shetland ponies, then?"

"Shaggier," he replied. "And coloured differently. Most are palomino, but others, more rarely, are spotted, almost like the dalmatian breed of dog."

He took a pipe from his pocket and, holding a match to it, pulled until it caught. "If you'll come over to the farm in the morning, we'll have a look at them." His gaze dropped to her slender legs, crossed carefully at the ankles. "I won't guarantee to find one tall enough for you to ride, but I think you'll be impressed anyway."

Greta laughed. "My students will love

hearing about your ponies. May I take pictures?"

"By all means. But tell me about your father's farm. Is grain a principal crop there as it is here?"

He had a way, Greta thought as she launched into a description of her Minnesota home, of making one feel important — the last quality she would have imagined in a man who was surely accustomed to being the center of attention wherever he went. But perhaps that was why he was so successful. He was able to draw others out, to make them speak and move as he directed.

All at once she found herself flushing, her words dying in her throat. Was that what Erik was doing? To amuse himself in Margit's absence, was he manipulating her as if she were one of his actresses? Surely he couldn't be all that interested in her brother's 4-H project and the Blue Earth County Fair.

"What is it?" he leaned toward her. "Have I asked too many questions?"

Greta started at the puzzled softness of his inquiry. It isn't that." She felt tongue-tied and foolish. "I'm boring you."

"Not at all." His brown hand came out and covered one of hers. "I would never allow that."

Sharp footsteps sounded in the hall and Margit entered the room. When she saw her fiancé and her cousin huddled together on the couch, she halted inside the doorway, her pale eyes jumping from Greta's flushed face to Erik bent beside her.

"What are you two talking about so earnestly?"

Greta felt her face go a deeper crimson, but Erik withdrew his hand and leaned back, seemingly unperturbed.

"Perhaps we'll tell you," he answered evenly, training a calm look on Margit's tense face, "but only after you first tell us what you've been talking about. And to whom."

Margit's delicate chin came up as she moved into the room. "Lily was on the phone." To Greta she said, "Lily is a seamstress in Visby. She's making my wedding dress — and your dress too. She's marvelous with a needle and she has the loveliest laces, which have been collected in her family for ages. If she's fond of a client, she sometimes offers them."

"Is she fond of you?" said Erik, who had risen and taken a position near the fireplace.

Margit barely looked at him. "I hope so. We'll know when we go for our fittings."

Greta got up, her heart pounding. She had renewed the friction between Margit and Erik, she feared and she was still shaken by the odd feeling that had come over her as he had listened to her talk.

Unable to meet his eyes, she focused instead on Margit. "I've suddenly realized how tired I am. I'll go up and get to bed if you don't mind."

"I do mind," said Margit, but instantly she covered her sharp answer with a smile. "I hate for this evening to end, but I know it must."

She turned to Erik, and Greta was struck with how small she looked, how fragile, next to Erik's towering strength.

"Greta has had a long journey. I'll say goodnight, too — if you'll forgive me — and see that she's properly tucked in."

"Of course." Erik's gaze stayed on her lifted face. "Shall I look for you both in the morning?"

"No, not in the morning. Birgitta and Karl will be showing us the shop."

"The shop isn't open on Saturday morning."

"Not usually," Margit retorted, "but Karl has just assured me that he'll be there." As soon as the words were out, she turned brick-red.

"Oh — Erik's gaze narrowed. "While you were talking to Lily, you managed to squeeze in a word with Karl too?"

"I just happened to think of calling him," Margit said quickly. "Since it was Saturday, I thought I'd better." She swallowed. "But we could have lunch with you afterward if you like. About one?"

Erik's gaze moved over her. "At one, then," he said finally. "I'll expect you."

Feeling ten again and like a prying snoop, Greta lingered in the doorway.

Was Erik going to kiss Margit?

For some ridiculous reason she wanted desperately to see him enfold Margit in his arms. It was all she could do to turn away and call back her good night from the hall-way.

Still standing apart from Margit, Erik followed her with his low-pitched voice. "Goodnight, Greta Lindstrom. Sleep well."

2

"**M**ARGIT — "

Greta turned with troubled eyes to her cousin, seated tailor-fashion on the bed. It was after eleven, but the two of them were still talking in Greta's cozy, dormered room tucked beneath the tiled roof of the farmhouse. "I feel I owe you an apology — or at least an explanation."

Margit yawned. "Really? What for?"

They had been whispering and giggling like children for more than an hour, and now here was Greta suddenly as serious as a judge.

"Did you break one of my dishes when you were helping Mother?" Margit teased.

Greta bit the corner of her lip. "Worse than that, I'm afraid. I think I offended you with the way I was speaking to Erik when you came into the sitting room."

"Oh, Greta, don't be silly!" Margit made a face. "Of course you didn't

28

offend me. Have you been thinking all this time that I was harboring bad feelings over that?"

"Well . . . you seemed a bit strained with Erik, and it wasn't his fault, I assure you."

"Was it your fault, then?" Margit said dryly. "Here on the eve of my wedding have you come to snatch my groom away?"

"Don't even tease about such a thing!"

Greta's normally untroubled brow furrowed in conscientious despair. "We were talking, that's all, and suddenly I had this strange feeling — " She hesitated and then plunged on. "I felt as if Erik — just for his own amusement and not from any real interest in me — might be leading me on, pulling information out of me about the farm and my family simply to see if he could."

Margit frowned. "Well, why shouldn't he?" She got up off the bed and came to put her arms around Greta's shoulders, bare in a filmy nightgown. "He's heard of you constantly for as long as he and I have known each other. But what he's heard has been my version of you.

Now I'm sure he wants to form his own opinion." She gave Greta a fond smile. "Which can't help but be wildly approving."

"Of course that's it, isn't it?" Greta rubbed her forehead ruefully. "All day I've had the most ridiculous sensations."

"Jet lag." Margit patted her arm. "Now don't think any more about it. Just crawl in bed and let me pull the covers up over you and turn out the light. We've talked far too long. I've worn you out."

Greta climbed obediently into bed, but as Margit reached for the light, she caught her hand. "You're not angry at Erik, then?"

Margit's eyes took on a guarded look. "Did I seem to be?"

"Not angry perhaps. Miffed might be a better word."

Margit shifted her gaze. "Erik annoys me sometimes. He's so possessive. Of course I should make allowances for that, I know. His experiences with women haven't always been happy ones, especially with Magro Pierre."

Greta tensed. "The actress in *Seasons of Torment?*"

30

Margit nodded. "I think she was the main reason he began retreating here so frequently."

"But if he's asked you to marry him, surely he's not still thinking of her!"

"I'm sure he isn't," Margit replied quickly. "It's just that he can't forget that I — " She broke off, flustered. "What I mean is, he must learn to trust me."

Greta put her arms around her cousin. "Erik already trusts you, Margit. He told me tonight that your straightforwardness was the quality that first attracted him to you." She lifted Margit's chin, urging a smile by smiling herself. "If he seems overly possessive, I'm sure it's only because he loves you so much."

To Greta's astonishment, Margit's face suddenly crumpled and she buried her face in her hands.

"What is it?" Greta asked in alarm. "What did I say?"

"Nothing — it's just that I'm such a silly fool." Margit lifted her face to give Greta a watery smile. "Bride's nerves," she offered weakly. "The closer the day comes, the more jittery I get."

She took the tissue Greta offered from

31

the box on the table and wiped her eyes. "Look at me. I've spoiled your arrival with my stupid tears. Can you ever forgive me?"

"We're sisters, aren't we?" Greta hugged her. "If we can't share our worries as well as our joys, then what do those hundreds of letters that have been flying over the Atlantic for fourteen years amount to?"

She took a tissue herself and blotted Margit's wet cheeks. "Naturally you're nervous. You're on the verge of becoming Mrs. Erik Lennart. In your place, I'd be paralyzed. It's good you cried," she said reassuringly. "You needed a release, and now you'll see how quickly your jitters vanish. Like mist."

Margit leaned against her. "You're so good for me, Greta. I knew you would be. I could never go through with this if you weren't here beside me."

"I'm here to stay," Greta soothed. "Until the knot is tied, I'll be here whenever you need me."

They kissed good night then, and Margit turned out the light. Greta settled back beneath the down comforter, feeling closer to Margit than she had ever felt. Her heart was bursting with love for her pale, beautiful cousin whose tears had wrung her heart.

But gradually her contentment left her. Sleep would not come, and finally she sat up, drawing her knees to her chest and staring through the partly opened window at the moonlight playing on the dormer.

What had Margit meant? "I could never go through with this if you weren't here . . . " As if the wedding were some sort of ordeal instead of a joyous, thrilling occasion. Even Erik had hinted at much the same thing when they met.

Jet lag, Greta thought again. She was reading double meanings into everything because she had passed through several time zones too quickly. Sleep. That was what she needed. A good night's sleep and tomorrow everything would be normal again.

She lay back down, but at once Erik's dark, brooding countenance presented itself. That stubborn sensuous mouth . . . the depthless eyes . . . the angular cheekbones that shadowed his face . . .

If only she could have seen him kiss Margit. How reassuring that would have been. Hazily she thought of the sleek Ferrari, of the huge diamond ring Margit wore. Things of substance, but not like a kiss . . .

Gradually she seemed lifted out of the room. She seemed to be floating and Erik was there beside her. In a moment, she came to with a jerk and sat up, panting. His lips had been pressed on hers, his arms had enfoldeld her. In her breast, her heart pounded from the force of his embrace, from his strong hands sliding possessively over her near-naked body.

Dry-mouthed, she switched on the light and stared around the room. The dresser and chair still stood where they had. Her robe lay over the foot of the bed. outside the window, crickets chirped and the moon hung low.

Sheepishly she snapped off the lamp and lay down again, reflecting on how easily the brain took hold of a waking thought and twisted it in sleep into a new form. But even as a heavy drowsiness settled back over her, a warning picked at a dark corner of her heart. She must never again allow herself to dream of Erik Lennart.

★ ★ ★

The studio-shop where Margit and two of her friends practiced their crafts and sold their wares was a tidy building that had once served as a barn. It was situated near the village of Gothem on an open plain and lay only a few miles from the Olsson farm.

Driving over to it in midmorning, Margit reminded Greta of the routine she normally observed and of which she had often written. Her custom was to work every weekday in the studio, taking turns with the others in waiting on the customers, who were mostly tourists. After her marriage, however, she said a little sadly, she would not be going there any more. She would keep the studio only until another artisan could be found to take up her rent.

"Erik has promised to outfit me with a studio in our own barn," she told Greta, "but I doubt if I'll be using it much."

"Why not?" said Greta, breathing

35

deeply of the fresh scents of pine and juniper that filled the golden morning. "He doesn't object to your working as a potter, does he?"

"Not really, but without Karl — and Birgitta . . . " Her voice trailed off. "Besides, I'll be busy with other things. Erik has a large house I must manage. And he has many friends." She swung a wan look around to meet Greta's blue eyes. "I must keep myself free to do whatever he wants."

Greta nodded, wondering, as they got out of the car, if Margit appreciated the security of her future. What must it be like to be loved by a man like Erik Lennart? To know that wealth and prestige and a comfortable home were soon to be yours and that whatever your needs, they would be quickly satisfied?

Feeling a trifle envious, she gave her attention to a question from Margit.

"What do you think of it?" her cousin asked, pointing to a wooden sign that hung over the door of a barn proclaiming Margit Olsson a potter, Birgitta Hedrin — who owned the building and lived in the adjacent farmhouse — a silversmith,

36

and Karl Korsmann, the lanky young man who appeared just then and greeted Greta curtly, a metal sculptor.

"I'm tremendously impressed," Greta said with enthusiasm. "Will you show me around?"

"We'll let Birgitta," Margit replied. "She owns the place."

But Birgitta, despite what Karl had told Margit on the telephone, had driven into Visby to the museum. In her stead, Karl himself led the way up the narrow stairs to the second floor, where the studios were and where he maintained his own bachelor apartment.

When they came down again, Greta commented on how tidy and spotless everything was. The wide windows that looked out onto a meadow where ripening barley swayed sparkled in the morning sun, and the display tables and shelves gleamed without a speck of dust.

Karl replied gruffly that he was the janitor, taking his wages as an even trade for the rent on his apartment.

From the other side of the room where she was rearranging several pieces of pottery, Margit said a bit sourly, "Karl is perfect for the job. He can't bear disorder — in anything."

The hostile glare that Karl returned sent a little shock zinging through Greta's veins. How did they all manage, she wondered, shut up in this tiny space if their temperaments conflicted? If she were Margit, she would be glad to get away to her own studio on Erik's farm.

But soon she forgot about everything except the enchantments the shop had to offer, and she moved from one area to another with growing admiration.

Margit's contributions — silkily glazed cups and pitchers, blue-gray bowls, and individually designed vases and containers — reflected the Nordic culture in their clean lines and muted color. Birgitta Hedrin's jewelry, laid out on black velvet in a long case toward the rear of the room, was both modern and ancient, the older-looking pieces being patterned after Viking treasures that the Gotland soil had recently yielded.

But it was Karl Korsmann's striking designs in dark metal hanging in the windows and from the ceiling that Greta found the most intriguing. Of the three, he had the greatest talent, she saw. However, the man himself was not nearly so impressive.

Karl's blond good looks she appreciated, but his disposition annoyed her. The wide, generous mouth that would have been virile and appealing had it turned up in a smile, he kept tightly clamped in a bitter line. As he moved about the shop a cloud of hostility surrounded him, and Greta thought uncomfortably that he took himself and his artistic temperament far too seriously to suit her tastes.

After a few minutes, in tones patently aimed for Greta's ears, he announced that he had a matter of importance to discuss with Margit. Quickly Greta excused herself, glad to get out into the sunshine. The strained atmosphere in the shop had depressed her, and she welcomed the pleasures of Birgitta's bright garden. The time passed quickly as she wandered from one neat little bed to the next, and she was surprised when Margit appeared and announced that it was past one o'clock.

"Erik will wonder what's happened to

us," Greta said as she crawled back into the Ferrari.

Margit replied grumpily, "I wish we hadn't promised to lunch with him."

"Why not? Has something gone wrong?" But Greta thought she knew the answer. Karl Korsmann's dark mood had transfered itself to Margit. "Did your friend upset you?"

"Not only me, but everything," Margit said grimly. "When Erik hears, he'll hit the ceiling."

"Can you tell me?"

"Of course. You'll find out soon enough anyway." Margit sighed. "It seems an Italian shop we've been dickering with for a while has finally decided to stock our things. Signora Valdetti's, in Venice."

"But that's wonderful," exclaimed Greta. "Isn't that what you once wrote you were dreaming of? Being represented in a good shop on the continent?" Greta frowned suddenly. "Or isn't it a good shop? Is that the problem?"

"It's an excellent shop." Margit turned the Ferrari up a birch-lined lane and shifted gears. "We couldn't ask for a finer place to begin building an international reputation. The trouble is, Birgetta and Karl have stockpiled for just such an event — and I haven't."

"What does that mean?"

"That they've worked double-time to build an inventory. But I've been busy with wedding plans. All I have on hand are those few pieces that you saw on the shelves."

"Oh, I see." Greta's gaze filled with sympathy. "Then you can't be a part of the arrangement. I don't blame you for being disappointed."

"If disappointment were all there were to it, I could handle that," said Margit. "But I can't fail Birgitta and Karl. This means too much to them, and Signora Valdetti has stipulated that it's all of us or nothing."

"Do you mean she won't take the metal designs and the jewelry unless she can have your pottery to? That's hardly fair is it?"

Margit shrugged. "She isn't interested in being fair. She wants variety for her shop — and she knows how to apply pressure to get it."

Greta's lips parted. "You're going to

comply with her wishes? But how can you
— unless she hasn't set a time limit?"

"She has. The end of the month. She's
demanding eight place settings in tones
of charcoal and blue on white, and she
wants all the extra pieces — platters,
bowls, a soup tureen, the lot."

"Can you do it?"

"Margit's small chin jutted out. "If I
work everyday."

"Then you can't have a wedding."

Margit turned on her fiercely. "Are
you going to fight me too? I have to
do this! And I can — if you help me
persuade Erik. And if you help me in
other ways too."

"I'll do anything I can." Greta saw how
near to tears Margit was and remembered
the scene last night in her bedroom. "But
I haven't any influence with Erik." Her
tone softened, and she laid a gentle hand
on Margit's arm. "Of course you want to
help your friends, but Erik has to come
first, doesn't he?"

Margit looked stricken. "The only way
he will be affected is that I'll have less
time to spend with him between now and
our wedding day." Her chin trembled.

"Why should he mind that when we'll be spending the rest of our lives together?"

From what she had seen of Erik the evening before, Greta felt certain that he would mind a great deal. And she agreed with him. Margit was sacrificing the most precious days of their courtship. How could she so lightly toss them aside?

But Margit's enthusiasm for her plan was growing. "Actually very little remains to be done in preparation for the wedding. The ceremony is to be at Erik's farm and his staff has taken over all the details for the reception — the flowers, the food, everything. The invitations are all ready, and my dress is almost done. There's really nothing left for me to do. The only thing that I really regret" — she bit her lip — "is that I'll lose so much time with you."

"Don't worry about that," Greta said, more cheerfully than she felt. "You and I can always sit up half the night and talk."

"Oh bless you!" Margit exclaimed, her smile breaking through. "I knew I could count on you. Now if only Erik will be half so generous."

★ ★ ★

The first glimpse of Erik's 'farmhouse' was a shock to Greta. Knowing that he was wealthy and prominent, she had expected something more elaborate than the ordinary cottages that dotted the landscape, but the tall, imposing ocher stucco that suddenly revealed itself through a thick clump of trees brought a gasp of astonishment from her lips.

Margit glanced across at her. "Hideous, isn't it?" she said with a smile when she saw Greta's look. "I don't know how I'll ever get used to it."

Greta was too amazed even to be polite. "I don't think it's hideous at all! I think it's the most wonderful house I've ever seen." She leaned forward in her seat, her eyes drinking in the lush formal garden that surrounded it, the quaint little balconies jutting from its upper stories, and the tidy row of dormers that footed the steep roof of the top floor. "It looks like a Hansel and Gretel cookie house!"

"Exactly," said Margit with a down-turning of her pretty mouth. "I wish it would crumble and disappear before I have to move into it."

Greta blinked, still unable to tear her eyes away from the dwelling that had instantly struck a note of longing in her. Oh, to call such a place one's home!

"Does Erik know you feel this way?"

Margit lifted her delicately arched brows. "He knows I prefer something more modern and less extravagant. To me, Birgitta's barn is much more appealing than this monstrosity."

"How unfortunate," Greta murmured, noticing the intriguing pebbled paths that circled the house and wound around to the gardens. To one side stood an arbor, cozy and inviting. On another side there were hothouses bursting with color. "I loved your studio . . . but this . . . " She brought a slender hand to her throat. "I can't imagine anyone who couldn't be happy here."

"You can't imagine me, then," Margit said crisply, and brought the car to a stop at the front door. She eyed it critically. "However, I do have plans for remodeling just as soon as Erik can be brought around."

45

Greta winced. Remodel this wonderful place? To anyone who cared for it that would be like cutting off an arm or a leg. Sympathy for Erik swept over her.

"Perhaps when you're living here — "

"I'll never like it," Margit said decisively. "But when it gets too unbearable, I suppose I can always retreat to Erik's Visby apartment or to his beach house at Botvadlvik. Any place but this!"

While Margit and Greta were talking, Erik himself appeared, coming from around the corner of the house with a large black dog that bounded toward Margit the moment she called its name.

"Tasha is the best friend I have," said Margit, pressing her fair cheek to the dog's silken ear. "Aside from you, of course," she added laughingly to Greta.

"Where do I fit in?" came Erik's cool voice.

"You?" Margit stood up. She was wearing tight-fitting white pants and a striped shirt that molded her high, firm breasts and emphasized her slender torso. "You're the lover," she said sharply, "or have you forgotten?"

For a moment the air hung frigid

between them, and Greta, her searching gaze going to Erik's stony countenance, was suddenly reminded of her dream.

Flushing, she turned away and said quickly, "I love your home, Erik. It's like a rare gem set in a perfect mounting."

"Or a Hansel and Gretel gingerbread house," Margit said cruelly, her eyes still on Erik's dark face. Then in swift apology she added, "I'm sorry. I sound like a fishwife."

"Or like someone bent on spoiling a beautiful day," Erik replied evenly. "What went wrong at the studio?"

How well he knows her! Greta thought, unable not to admire Erik's perceptiveness, but on the other hand, feeling a bit sorry for her cousin too. Surely there was a subtler way Margit could have led up to the unpleasant news she must break to Erik than to begin their meeting with a quarrel.

Margit, however, knew how to use her blond charm. Reaching out, she took one of Erik's arms and tucked her hand into the crook of his elbow, pulling him close enough for a swift kiss on the cheek.

"Do you have spies everywhere,"

she teased huskily, "that you are so knowledgeable about what you couldn't possible know?"

"What is it that I can't possibly know?" he demanded gruffly, but Greta could see that Margit's affectionate gesture had melted some of his reserve.

"Can't it wait to tell you until later? After we've had some of cook's delicious lobster bisque with a glass of champagne?" Margit smiled beguilingly up into his face. "We shouldn't spoil that, should we?"

Won over, Erik suggested that they tour the gardens before going in. "There's a species of moss rose in full bloom now that will be closed in a hour," he said. "I want you both to see it."

"And the *russ*," Greta reminded, falling into step beside them. "Don't forget you've promised to show me your herd too."

Margit rolled her eyes. "Have no fear. No one escapes from Erik's farm without admiring the ponies and the four-horned rams as well."

Greta had never heard of rams with double sets of horns, and immediately

Erik launched into an enthusiastic description of them and the sensation they created each time he showed them at a fair. Over lunch, served on a shaded terrace at the back of the house, he elaborated further.

"I have fifteen of them now," he said between sips of the bisque and morsels of crisp salad a pretty young maid had set before them on fine china plates. "We're breeding them as we are the *russ,* and with the same purpose in mind — to keep them from dying out. They're a native species, you see, with two thick horns curling up and two thinner ones, like sword blades, curving down. Occasionally one will even develop six horns."

"They really belong in a carnival," Margit quipped, but then she added quickly, "No — quite seriously, Erik is doing a necessary work in preserving the breed. They aren't to be found in other countries, and if it weren't for his efforts, they soon wouldn't be found here either."

"Erik regarded her with a thin smile and turned his attention back to the meal, but Greta saw by the way his shoulders relaxed that Margit's comments had pleased him.

He is like a fine musical instrument, she mused as she sipped from her champagne glass. He responds to the slightest variation in tone . . . to the briefest look. Covertly she studied his dark head, turned now with a question for Margit. His sensitivity was what made him an outstanding director, she knew, but it in no way detracted from the rugged virility that one could not fail to be aware of the moment one saw him. Even with a touch as innocent as the one with which he had covered her hand the evening before he had the power to produce an immediate sensual reaction.

Greta shifted uneasily in her chair, recalling once more the daze in which she had awakened from her dream, actually believing for an instant that Erik had kissed her . . . held her . . .

"Greta!" Margit's playful smile revealed a row of pearly teeth. "Where have you gone? Back to Minnesota?"

Greta started, blushing. "Forgive me. I was woolgathering, I'm afraid."

"Delectable wool it must have been,"

Erik replied in the resonant voice that never failed to send a tingling excitement coursing through her. "Do you see the stars in her eyes, Margit?"

"There are always stars in my cousin's eyes," Margit answered fondly. "Greta is an idealist, Erik. A dreamer." Then wickedly she added, "I told you yesterday she was dreaming of you, didn't I?"

"Margit!" Greta turned crimson.

"It's true, Erik," Margit went on unrelentingly. "Before she came, she had you pictured in a dozen ways, she told me."

Erik's amused gaze moved over Greta's flushed face. "Do I measure up to any one of them now?" he asked quietly. "I would hate not to be true to at least one image you hold of me."

"I expected you to be fair-skinned," Greta replied weakly.

Her remark increased his amusement, and he exchanged smiles with Margit. "When you've been here a little longer, you'll see that not every Swede is taffy blond," he commented dryly. "Particularly one whose grandmother was Italian."

At the mention of the word 'Italian,'

Margit's face lost its gaiety, but Greta, failing to make the connection between Erik's grandmother and the Venetian signora who had upset Margit's day, thought only that Margit was tiring of the subjects she already knew enough about. Nevertheless, she could not resist one more question of Erik.

"How did it happen that your grandfather chose a bride with a Mediterranean background?"

"He went *a-viking*," Erik replied, and then, when he saw her puzzled look, went on to explain. "Plundering — that's what *viking* originally meant. Except that my grandfather was plundering the tapestry market for his export business when he met my grandmother — making him, I suppose a rather modern Viking, but a fairly typical one at that, as far as Gotlanders are concerned anyway. Our countrymen of old were principally interested in trading instead of raiding, and fortunately, for them at least, that attitude helped make them the richest Vikings of all."

He found his pipe in the pocket of his jacket and struck a match to it. "At least my grandfather certainly considered the prize he brought home the richest treasure of his life."

Margit came into the conversation with a brittle smile and a tartness in her voice that contrasted sharply with the drowsy afternoon and the pleasant ease with which Erik had been describing his ancestry.

"All this talk of Italy," she said a trifle too loudly, "brings me to my subject."

Greta flinched, but Erik seemed unperturbed, as if in his mind everything that had gone before had only been leading up to this moment. "What subject is that, Margit?"

"My problem," she said staunchly. "I mentioned it earlier."

"Oh, yes — " He drew deeply on his pipe and then exhaled. "The thing that went wrong at the studio."

Margit swallowed and put on a smile. The gesture seemed to give her courage, and after a faltering start, she went on in a more precise manner to inform him of Signora Valdetti's offer to place the work of her and her partners in the Venetian shop. When she was finished,

Greta realized that throughout the whole recital she had been holding her breath. She let it out quietly and waited.

"So you see," Margit concluded, "I have no choice, Erik. It's absolutely necessary that I do this work, and that I get started on it immediately."

For a long moment Erik looked at her, his face an unreadable mask. Finally he said softly, "No one is stopping you."

Margit, who could not hide her surprise that he had not exploded, was flabbergasted.

"You don't mind?" She leaned toward him, taking his hand, her pale eyes earnestly entreating. "Really, Erik, you must tell me how you feel."

"I wasn't aware that it mattered how I feel."

Stung by the sudden iciness of his tone, Margit took her hand away. "That's unfair. Of course your feelings matter."

"Then I'm sure you considered them when you made up your mind before you came here." His voice was razor-edged. "Therefore, the question being a moot one, I suggest we drop it."

Staring at her empty champagne glass,

Greta wished she were anywhere but seated on this sunny terrace. But she stayed where she was, realizing that to excuse herself at this point would only call attention to her presence. If only I could simply vanish! she thought in anguish.

Suddenly Margit pushed back her chair and stood up, her light-colored eyes blazing. "I counted on you for understanding, Erik!"

Greta was appalled. That wasn't true — and Erik surely knew it! Margit had dreaded the encounter for the very reason that Erik would *not* understand. It was obvious now that she had deliberately played up to him while they ate, hoping to soften the blow, and now she was attempting to shift the burden of her guilt onto him. For the first time since she had known Margit, Greta felt a moment of intense dislike. It quickly passed, however, when she saw how close Margit was to tears.

Taking a quavering breath, Greta said quietly, "I realize this is not my business, but perhaps the opinion of an objective third party may fill a need here."

Margit's brimming eyes and Erik's smoldering ones turned on her simultaneously. Her mouth went dry, but she went on bravely.

"You're angry with each other because each of you feels slighted." She paused, wondering if she dared go on. "Margit, because she is involved in a situation not of her own making but one that demands her loyalty. And you, Erik" — Greta found it enormously difficult to meet his gaze — "you resent being cheated out of precious moments you might have spent with Margit before your marriage."

Greta passed the tip of her tongue over her parched lips. "Neither reason would matter at all if you didn't love each other." Again she paused and searched their tense faces. "Isn't that the most important thing?"

A heavy silence came down over the table, and Greta wished fervently she could drop into one of the cracks between the flagstones.

Finally Erik spoke. "My apologies, Margit. Naturally you must not renege on your friends."

"You understand then?" Tears trembled

on the tips of Margit's eyelashes. "You do see that this isn't something I'm doing just because I want to? I must!"

He held on to his arctic reserve. "Then I applaud your determination to honor your obligations."

For an instant Margit stood uncertainly beside the table, but all at once she leaned forward. Cupping Erik's strong chin in her curved palm, she kissed him full on the lips. Then she turned and ran across the terrace, disappearing into the shadowy interior of the house.

Greta rose hurriedly. "I interfered. I'm sorry, Erik."

"You needn't be. He got up, and Greta was appalled at the weariness that showed on his face. There was still, however, a forcefulness about him, an innate assurance that made her wonder if, in Margit's place, she would have dared provoke him.

"None of this was your doing," he said. "As a matter of fact, you saved the day." Jamming his hands into his pockets, he added harshly, "The wedding day, I mean."

Greta caught her breath. "Oh, no

— Margit would never have called off the wedding over such a trifle."

"But *I* might have." His brown eyes surveyed her with calculating coolness. "And I don't for a minute agree that Margit's stand represented a trifle." His gaze narrowed. "I thought it more of a showdown. A pitting of the wills."

A sinking sensation took over Greta's stomach. If that was what had taken place here, she should have kept out of it entirely.

"Oh, Erik, don't be angry with Margit. Without realizing she had done so, she laid a pleading hand on the warm skin of his arm.

A muscle leaped along his jawline. "Yes, Greta?"

Instantly she snatched her hand back, two bright spots of color leaping into her cheeks. He had spoken with infinite courtesy, but irony edged his words, and Greta felt all at once as if she were a member of a conspiracy to undermine whatever was left of Erik Lennart's regard for the feminine sex. Margo Pierre, Margit, and now me. She cringed. All of us out to deceive him.

58

But suddenly she raised her head defiantly. She spoke softly, but her voice rang out with authority on the quiet terrace. "I suppose what it all boils down to is whether you love Margit enough to accept her judgment as equal to your own."

They stared at each other. Greta clenched her teeth to keep them from chattering and watched a pulse hammer at the curve of Erik's tanned throat.

"I don't follow your meaning," he said flatly.

"I think you do." Greta was amazed at her nerve. "Margit has opinions. Loyalties, as you put it. She will always have — just as you will. Marriage won't change that in either of you. If you can't accept independence in a woman" — she swallowed, terrified now by the thin ice she was skating on — "then I think it's possible you're marrying the wrong one."

The roar of an expensive engine booming to life in the background shattered the silence between them. The sound accelerated, echoed around the corners of the mansion, and then faded as the car sped down the drive.

When the air was still again, Erik fixed a contemptuous gaze on Greta's astonished face.

"Your dear cousin, whom you have so eloquently defended, has just driven off and left you. What is your opinion of that particular act of independence?"

3

AFTER the first numbing moment when Greta realized that Margit had actually abandoned her to the caustic mercies of her fiancé, panic engulfed her. Then suddenly she was reminded of the dozens of playground battles she had witnessed as a teacher, and the humor of her current situation struck her.

She and Erik were like two angry children squared off against each other. Margit's victims, left to hack out this embarrassing predicament as best they could while Margit, who had started it all, had speedily removed herself.

A disarming smile broke over Greta's face. "Margit, it seems, is quite professional at making an exit."

The unexpectedness of the remark caught Erik unprepared, but an instant later his own smile replaced the look of tight reserve that had masked his face.

"I suppose we do look pretty silly

glaring at each other, don't we?"

Greta laughed. "I feel silly enough."

"So do I — and there's nothing I detest more." With a disturbing intensity, his gaze focused on her upturned lips. "What shall we do about it?"

"Well — " Greta thought for a moment, then sheepishly she eyed the untouched dessert plate on the table. "If you don't mind, to begin with, I'd like a strawberry tart."

Erik's lips twitched. Leaning over, he brought the plate up from the table. "Try a chocolate eclair, too, why don't you?"

Relieved at being able to put unpleasantness behind them, they sat down together and with a kind of greedy abandon attacked the divine midget morsels Erik's pastry cook had concocted, Greta declaring finally that she was awarding the lemon-filled squares a blue ribbon for distinctive quality.

In response Erik, who was once again the relaxed assured host, popped the last one on the plate into his mouth, smiled his approval, and then naughtily licked his fingers.

"Come along," he said rising. "Since

your cousin has left me in charge for the afternoon, let's go and have a look at the rams and the *russ*. Then I want to show you the rye crop — the best this land has ever produced, I'm told." He took hold of her arm. "Afterward, if you still have the energy, we'll take a turn through the woods on horseback.

★ ★ ★

At five, exhausted from a tour of Erik's fields, woods, and pastures, they returned to the house, and Greta collapsed on a sofa in the comfortable old study Erik used as an office.

Still in the mellow mood the jaunt around the farm had produced, Erik went to the bar to fill two glasses with sherry, leaving Greta free to admire the room. The walls were paneled in a glowing hardwood on one side and on the other, opposite wide windows, floor-to-ceiling shelves stretched. An enviable number of handsome leather-bound books were arranged there as well as objects of art evidently collected from numerous points around the globe. There were jade bookends, cloisonné vases, a stone face with definite Mayan features, black stinkwood carvings from Africa, and a dozen more pieces that, given the time, Greta would eagerly have examined more closely.

It was Erik, however, who captured her attention as he came to sit beside her. She saw at once that his mood had changed with the chameleonlike swiftness she had noticed in him before, and her heart sank. It had been such a lovely afternoon, but her intuition told her it was about to be spoiled.

"Shall I tell you," he began in the tone she had dreaded, "the real reason I became so angry with Margit?"

Their hours together had passed without a single mention of the unpleasant incident at lunch, but Greta saw there was no chance of averting it now.

"If it's important for you to tell me," she agreed reluctantly, "then please do."

"You touched on it yourself," he began, twirling the stem of his sherry glass. "When you said that I object to being cheated out of precious hours with Margit before our marriage. But that's only the tip of the iceberg." He lifted a pair of watchful eyes. "What concerns me more is that I am beginning to wonder if she and I have the same ideas about what makes a marriage work."

Greta's heart sank, but she did her best to hide her distress. "Oh, I'm sure you do," she said lightly. "If not, Margit would not have agreed to become your wife."

He answered stubbornly. "Perhaps she hasn't given the proper amount of thought to it."

"Perhaps she doesn't need to," Greta countered, desperately eager to convince herself as well as Erik. The wedding day was less than a month off. As Margit had said, all the preparations had been made. Now if Erik were having second thoughts . . . The possibility was too upsetting even to consider.

As if he read her thoughts, Erik said curtly, "in any case, however, we'll carry on with our plans. There's no question about that."

"No, of course not," Greta answered evenly, but it was all she could do not to voice her relief.

Erik looked steadily at her. "I realize how fortunate I am to have found Margit. No doubt we'll have our share of problems, but we'll iron them out somehow."

"As all couples do," offered Greta encouragingly.

Erik's sensuous mouth turned down wryly. "A great many couples these days resort to the divorce court when the going gets rough, but Margit and I will not be among those. 'For better or for worse' is not a phrase I take lightly."

He finished the last of his sherry and set the glass aside with an annoying air of superiority she had not noticed before. He seemed, in fact, an entirely different man from the relaxed, comfortable companion he had been all afternoon.

"When Margit is a few years older," he said decisively, "she will realize that the kind of marriage her parents have — the kind my grandparents enjoyed for fifty-two years — is the most important relationship two human beings can cultivate."

Greta felt a prickle of irritation rise along the back of her neck. "I don't see that age has anything to do with appreciating that."

"Don't you?" Barely concealed condescension colored his tone. "That may be because you and Margit are both only twenty-four."

Greta had not been aware that he knew her age, and she found the fact that he had called attention to it oddly unsettling.

Erik went on. "Starry-eyed, full of romantic illusions," he said with a touch of scorn. "It's difficult for women as young as you and Margit to realize that such things are of little importance in a lasting relationship."

"You're contradicting yourself," said Greta, trying to keep her annoyance from showing. "Yesterday you were admiring Kenneth and Hannah's romantic walks."

"You misunderstood." His keen gaze traveled over her. "I was admiring the feeling of companionship that exists between them."

A coldness clutched Greta's heart. "Is it your opinion that companionship is all they share?"

Erik laughed unpleasantly. "You may

draw your own conclusions there. I have no intention of speculating about the private feelings of my future in-laws."

What about your own private feelings? The chill around Greta's heart deepened. Everything was beginning to come clear now. It was no wonder that from the start she had sensed between Margit and Erik a flatness where there should have been sparkle, indifference instead of enthusiasm. She could see now that Erik's previous experiences with women — Margo Pierre in particular, probably — had left him jaded and cynical. Secretly she had felt that Margit was a bit too blasé where her handsome fiancé was concerned, but perhaps her cousin was behaving in the only way the pride of a woman in love would allow in such a situation — with a cynicism of her own.

A sick feeling took hold of Greta. What kind of life could Margit hope for with this man who appeared to have turned thumbs down on the passion and fire that any young bride had a right to expect in a new husband?

Her gaze leaped to the lean, virile figure of Erik as he filled their glasses again with sherry, and a shiver swept over her. The excitement he was so plainly capable of arousing with even the most ordinary movements of his athletic, sensuous form would make life all the more unbearable for the woman he married if he turned a cold shoulder to her.

Greta's heart ached for Margit, and her fingers trembled as she took the glass from Erik's outstretched hand.

But as he stared down at Greta, the glazed look his face had taken on while he talked faded, and he said with some warmth she had been drawn to as he showed her around the farm, "My philosophizing about marriage has upset you, hasn't it?"

Why deny it? She lowered her eyes. "I want my cousin to be happy."

"Married to me, you don't think she will be?"

"I'm not sure now."

Erik studied her in silence. Then he sat down across from her. He put his glass on a low table, and folding his tanned arms over the suede vest that hung loosely from his shoulders, he said quietly, "I admire your courage in telling me that."

There was nothing in his voice that was condescending or arrogant or annoyingly assured as there had been moments before. Greta lifted her eyes and saw that the same was true of his face. The expression that lay there now was the same forthright one he had worn most of the afternoon, the look that had made her feel she had known him all her life. A little of her resistance melted.

"Perhaps I'm being unfair."

"Perhaps you are," he murmured absently. "Or perhaps I am." His gaze moved over the books on his shelves and finally came back to rest on Greta's parted lips and anxious eyes. "I want Margit to be happy too. She will be. I promise you that."

A startling thought flashed across Greta's mind. He was an actor as well as a director. A vignette as vivid as if it were taking place right there in the room sprang up inside her head. Erik with Margit in his arms, passionately caressing her . . . holding her so closely that Greta's throat closed convulsively.

A torrent of mixed emotions welled up inside her. If Erik chose, *when* he chose, he could make Margit exquisitely happy, but it would all be a sham, a polished performance by one who had every skill in perfect control, but felt no love. Greta uttered a choked sound.

Erik's brows jumped together. "What is it?"

Her stark gaze met his. "Not all fairy tales have happy endings, do they?"

Whether he caught her meaning or not, Greta was not to know. A shocking peal sounded from the doorbell, and then in a moment Margit breezed into the study, cheeks aglow, her blond fair fetchingly disarranged by the wind.

"So you two are still here," she exclaimed. "As solemn as a pair of old owls. Have you sat here all afternoon thinking what a wretched, spoiled brat I am to have spoiled our lovely luncheon?"

Not waiting for an answer, she swooped down on Erik, perching on the arm of his chair and taking his wide shoulders in a affectionate hug that ended with her lips trailing along the angle of his cheekbone.

"What a delicious smell you have, Erik.

Juniper and fresh air and . . . Ummm, what's this?" In a provocative gesture that made Greta blush, she put the tip of her tongue to the corner of his lips. "Sugar and lemon?" She sent a mischievous, accusing look flying between Erik and Greta. "You've buried your dismay by stuffing yourselves full of cook's lemon squares, and I'll bet anything you haven't saved a one for me."

Greta stared at Margit, overwhelmed by her frantic gaiety. What had happened to skyrocket her into such jubilance? Or was it only a pose?

Erik was the first to speak. "For your information, we haven't sat here all afternoon," he said, dryly. "While you've been off throwing your pots, we've covered every inch of the farm. Now we're trying to relax, and you come storming in with enough energy for all three of us." He squeezed Margit's shoulders as if never a cross word had passed between them. "What is there in that clay you use that always ignites you so?"

"You should throw a pot and find out for yourself," she answered impishly. "Now, Greta, what are you thinking behind that disapproving scowl? Are you still furious at me for behaving so stupidly at lunchtime?"

"No, of course not." But Greta felt as stunned as if a brick had dropped on her head. The lightning-quick changes of mood these two displayed were too much for her. Since Margit's arrival, the things Erik had told her had taken on a dreamlike quality. The man gazing with such obvious affection into Margit's flushed face could not be the same coldly reserved one who had so recently and clearly intimated that romance had no place in his life. His hands sliding down Margit's arms spoke louder than words ever could.

Greta got up dizzily. "I'm afraid I've overstayed my welcome. Erik has been entertaining me for hours. Please point me in the direction of the farm, and I'll walk along home."

"After our horseback ride?" Erik snorted. "You wouldn't make it as far as the first gate."

But Greta was firm. "You two will want some time alone."

Margit spoke up with unexpected

73

candor. "Yes, we will. There's no hurry, of course, but when you're ready to leave, I've left the keys in the Ferrari. Erik is coming to supper so he can drive me over."

Greta realized that Margit was politely pushing her out of the house, but she was so eager to be gone herself that she felt only relief.

Out in the fresh, clear air she breathed deeply, trying to shake off the mixture of odd feelings at war within her. She loved Margit, but she was discovering that her beautiful cousin was a far more complicated creature than she had ever imagined — and as for Erik, that contradictory, magnetic man who exercised such a strange power over her that he even invaded her dreams — Her pulse quickened. She had no idea what she felt about him.

★ ★ ★

Despite Margit's maneuverings, she and Erik spent less than an hour alone. Before six they came up the lane in Erik's red Porsche, Margit still in high good humor.

74

Erik's mood was not so exuberant, but reflected a kind of speculative watchfulness that sent uneasy prickles up Greta's spine each time their glances met.

What was he thinking?

Who was the real Erik Lennart? she wondered. That aloof, withdrawn stranger following her with his eyes? Or the relaxed, disarming man with whom she had spent the afternoon?

While Greta was occupied with her thoughts, Margit's chatter dominated the supper table. Afterward, while Kenneth and Hannah went for their walk, she and Erik drew Greta out onto the front steps for a talk.

"Everything is going to work out so beautifully, Greta," Margit began with the same high-pitched excitement she had exhibited during the meal. "As Erik said at lunch, he understands why I must work hard for the next few weeks — and I, in turn, understand how much at loose ends he'll be while I'm busy."

She took Greta's hands in hers and trained her irresistibly pale look on Greta's wary countenance. Greta had seen that look at noon and dreaded what it might be the foreruner of.

"Both of us understand," Margit went on decisively, "how special it is that you've come to Gotland to share our joy, and so" — a dazzling smile turned up her lips — "while you're here, we will not have you bored for one single minute."

"Bored?" Greta felt herself being crowded into a corner. "Whatever gave you the idea I'd be bored?"

"I'll be away all day at my studio," Margit said. "Father and Mother will be busy with the farmwork — "

"I can help, can't I?" said Greta indignantly. "After all, I've had enough experience to be of some use milking cows and driving tractors and cooking — "

Margit's eyes snapped. "All the more reason for you not to spend your holiday stuck out here doing them for us! You are going to see Gotland as a visitor should, and Erik" — she took his arm possessively — "Erik is going to show it to you."

"No, I couldn't impose in that way!" Greta came to her feet as if shot from a cannon. "It's thoughtful of you both to want to entertain me," she said hastily, "and I do appreciate your concern." She raised both hands to ward off their objections. "But I'm not a guest. I'm a member of the family. There's a bicycle in the barn. Between chores I can show myself the island."

"Do you imagine that you can bicycle all the way to Visby?" demanded Margit.

"Of course."

"Not on *my* old ten-speeder!"

Erik spoke up brusquely. "It's not a question of whether you can or you can't. The point is that it will be my pleasure to show Gotland to you."

With a peculiar thud of her heart, Greta heard the persuasive resonance of his voice. Fighting the spell it cast over her, she said with less firmness than she would have liked, "You're kind, but I couldn't put you to that much trouble."

Erik eyed her with taunting amusement. "Am I to interpret your reluctance to mean that the three hours we spent together this afternoon were all you can take of my company?"

"You know that's not true!" Under his sardonic scrutiny Greta felt her resistance crumbling, though all her instincts warned her not to give in.

Margit was quick to see her wavering and pounced upon it. "It's all settled, then."

"We start first thing in the morning," said Erik, rising abruptly. "But in an academic way to begin with. One can't tour Gotland without knowing its history first, so we'll start in my library at nine sharp." He feigned the look of a strict headmaster. "The first lesson will focus on the Hanseatic League."

"The what?" stammered Greta.

"There, you see?" Erik shrugged and lifted his brows at Margit. "Ignorance personified. She may need a week in the schoolroom before she can be trusted to properly appreciate the wonders of our Baltic paradise." His cool look went back to Greta. "Get a goodnight's sleep," he murmured. "And bring a notebook in the morning."

★ ★ ★

Morning came too soon for Greta, but she was too nervous to lie in bed restlessly tossing. When she heard Hannah below going out to milk, she rose and followed her out to the barn.

Afterward, the two of them fixed a hearty breakfast, which Kenneth ate hungrily. Greta, however, barely picked at hers and Margit, whose exuberance seemed to have evaporated during the night, asked listlessly for a glass of milk and then drove off to her studio.

Hannah bristled with disapproval as the car disappeared down the lane. "There's not a bit of point to any of it," she said to Greta while they tidied up the kitchen. "Margit should be preparing herself for the wedding and giving Erik her time instead of shutting herself up all day in that barn. I don't like it. Not one bit."

Unwilling to take sides, Greta nevertheless offered what she meant to be a soothing remark. "She feels a loyalty to Birgitta and Karl."

"Karl!" Hannah replied tartly. "She owes nothing to him. It's Erik she ought to be thinking of. He's a restless kind of man," she went on in her plain way. "He's seen a lot of the world, and he isn't one who'll put up with too much if it doesn't suit him. If Margit doesn't watch her step, he might just up and go back to Stockholm if he takes a notion."

But she seemed to remember then that it was Greta she was scolding and not Margit, who — deserved it, and she put her arms affectionately around the shoulders of her young cousin and said fondly, "But as long as it has to be, I'm glad it's you who'll be occupying Erik's time."

Greta had laughed then. But she wasn't laughing now as she looked into the mirror in her dormered bedroom and saw with dismay the tightness around her mouth and the strain that showed too plainly in her eyes.

It was stupid to feel so uneasy, she reproached herself. Erik would give her a few geography lessons, show her the sights, and that would be it. Margit had instigated the arrangement and it had been blessed by her mother. What was there to worry about?

Still the butterflies batted about in her stomach. One minute she felt comfortable and assured in Erik's presence, and the next her every nerve was on edge. His dark eyes taunted her. Even when she was apart from him, she remembered the way his mouth turned up in that slow, compelling smile, the touch of his hand on her elbow, the smell of his sun-warmed skin . . .

It would have been better, she admitted, giving way to the smothering sensation in her chest, if she had never come to Gotland. If she had stayed in Minnesota, she would have known Erik only as Margit's handsome husband, whom she read about in Margit's letters. She could have gone on picturing him in the same glamorous, enchanted way she had done when she first heard of him. And Margit and herself could have remained the ideal sisters who had learned to love each other through their correspondence. She might never have discovered Margit's selfishness or the quicksilver changes of mood that sometimes baffled and dismayed her.

Greta longed to know again the joy and eagerness she had felt stepping off the ferry in Visby, but what she experienced most often now was apprehension and an indefinable yearning that unsettled her.

"Wearying suddenly of the arguments that had besieged her since dawn she snatched up the note book Erik had ordered and cast a final glance at herself in the mirror.

Slim, straight skirt curving over narrow hips. Soft white shirt molding her breasts discreetly . . . sandals . . . scarf. She was ready.

But for what? her reflection challenged.

Licking her lips to ward off the panic that threatened to overwhelm her, Greta pulled her eyes away from the mirror and hurried down the stairs.

.4

WITHIN a few days after the start of her sessions with Erik, Greta had relaxed to the extent that she could look back on her unsettled state that first morning with an indulgent smile.

Erik had put her at ease at once with a well-planned program of information. Though on the fringes of her consciousness she was still very much aware of his powerful physical attractiveness, now his personality intrigued her too. He was an interesting, highly intelligent man, and when she concentrated on that aspect of him, she found it not too difficult to push into the background any unacceptable emotions his nearness might arouse.

She had discovered that his theatrical experiences enabled him to bring a richness to any subject. He was witty, he had a beguiling sense of humor that never failed to surprise her when it made itself known, and he seemed genuinely interested in helping her to appreciate Gotland as he knew and loved it. His excellence as a teacher was unparalleled, and the hours she spent with him flew by.

Towards the end of the week, however, Greta innocently began a conversation that broke the calm of the days that had preceded it.

"You should apply at Lindberg Academy," she teased, naming the school where she taught. "The history department would snatch you up for its middle-school boys in a minute, and think how much more rewarding dodging spitwads in the corridors would be than soothing temperamental actresses."

"I don't doubt that," Erik answered with the first note of bitterness she had heard from him since they had begun their lessons in his cozy study. "You have no idea how that world disgusts me when I think of it now," he said.

"The film world?" Regretting that she had spoiled their ordinarily pleasant coffee break on the sunny terrace, she searched her mind for a suitable change of subject.

But Erik went on. "Tinsel and glitter. Plastic smiles and cheap emotions." He snorted in disgust. "I've had enough of those to last me forever."

Greta bent to smell a bouquet of roses in the center of the table and then cast a sidewise glance at him. The coldness in his eyes, which moments before had glowed with enthusiasm as he spoke about the voyages of the Vikings, dismayed her, but Erik's past intrigued her, too, particularly since he seemed so intent on putting it behind him forever.

She made her tone deliberately light. "It can't have been all that bad, can it?" Though Erik could be moody and sometimes curt and arrogant, there was about him a determination to rend from every moment everything that it had to offer. Greta herself shared this zest for living, and she felt secure enough in their new relationship to challenge him.

She felt secure in their routine too. In the mornings they studied. They broke around ten and again at lunchtime, most often eating on the terrace in the company of Tasha, Erik's black hound. In the afternoon Erik took her to the spots on the island where history had actually been made and then later they rode, or Greta watched while Erik worked with his delightful wild ponies. When Margit appeared at five, Greta lingered for only a few minutes, leaving them alone while she walked leisurely back to the Olsson farm along the green-bordered lanes, taking pleasure in the glorious golds and silvers of the dying afternoons.

Now Greta gazed frankly at Erik and was reminded with a faint stab of envy of how lucky Margit was. Erik was exhilarating company and every day she found herself eager to know him better.

"You must have found some kind of satisfaction in making those wonderful films," she told him. "How many were there? Seven?"

He swung his head around. "You've kept count?"

"Naturally. You aren't exactly unknown, my friend."

He gave her a thoughtful look. "Even on a Minnesota farm?"

"Well, why not?" Greta was mildly indignant. "Minnesota, despite what you may think to the contrary, is not the end of the earth."

But Erik did not respond to her sarcasm. In a serious tone he said, "I suppose I've never thought much about who was viewing my films. I've never thought, for example, in specifics — of persons like your father and mother stepping out on a Saturday night half a world away to see *Seasons of Torment.*

"I hate to disillusion you," Greta said with a mischievous twinkle, "but if I'm not mistaken my parents watched that particular one on the *Friday Night Big Show* right in our own living room."

Unexpectedly Erik chuckled. "You love to puncture my ego, don't you?"

It was Greta's turn to be surprised. "Do I? I wasn't aware of that."

"Oh, come now. When you tripped me up yesterday on the Rhine trade routes, I saw that vindictive glint in your beautiful blue eyes."

It was the first time he had commented on her looks since he had compared them to Margit's the day they met, and Greta felt an alarming increase in her pulse rate. *Your beautiful blue eyes . . .*

Flustered, she steered the conversation back to movie-making. "Seriously, Erik. Isn't there a great deal more to directing than being annoyed by the superficial aspects that sometimes mar it?"

The keenness of his look was disconcerting. "Do you really want to get into this?"

"Yes — " She brought her chin up. "If you don't object."

"Why?"

"Because it's interesting. And because it puzzles me how you could simply abandon a career in which you were so successful."

"Perhaps I've learned to measure success differently than I did when I was younger."

"You put a great deal of emphasis on age, don't you?" The remark came out more sharply than Greta intended, and she tempered it quickly with a smile. "What I mean is, you seem to think Margit and I are mere children at twenty-four while you at" — she raised her shoulders in a questioning gesture — "at thirty-three? — are an ancient sage."

Erik observed her thoughtfully. "I'm thirty-five."

Greta shrugged. "So what?"

The flip response amused him. "I've seen eleven more years of life than you."

Greta answered huffily. "Were your eyes open all the time?"

"You're determined to rile me, aren't you?"

"I'm determined to make you tell me the truth." Greta was amazed and even a little annoyed at her own persistence, and yet for a reason she couldn't define, she seemed unable to let go of the subject.

"You can't make me believe," she went on, "that this farm, as charming as it is, is enough for you. That you don't still long now and then to be back in that other world, no matter how artificial it seems."

His answer came with shocking abruptness. "We've said quite enough on this subject, I think."

The inscrutable expression he turned on her caught Greta off-guard, but her response popped out before she could stop it. "Why? Because you're afraid to admit that I'm right?"

"I'm a farmer now," he said harshly.

"Wonderful — farming is a great life. But it needn't require that you close your mind to everything else that once interested you."

"What business is that of yours?" he snapped.

Greta sat back, as stunned as if he had slapped her. Worse she could give him no answer. He was right. How he felt about his former career really wasn't any of her affair. Through a tight throat she said quietly, "I'm sorry, Erik. I don't know what got into me. Please forgive me."

She saw the muscles in his cheek ridge. He got up. "Shall we go in?"

Feeling as embarrassed as a scolded child, she pushed back her chair, but when they were in the library again, Erik astonished her by saying offhandedly, "I have a small projection room upstairs. Later, if you'd like, we can look at some clips that ended up on the cutting-room floor instead of the screen."

"I would like that." Her heart turned over. "I'd like that very much."

"Then I'll have them set up," he

answered, pressing a button on his desk to summon a servant.

After that, they concentrated on the foreign merchants who had taken over Visby in the fourteenth century, but Greta found her thoughts straying repeatedly to the unexpected treat he had offered her, and she looked forward eagerly to the afternoon.

★ ★ ★

The 'small' projection room Erik had spoken of was not small at all in Greta's opinion. It occupied most of one end of the house's third floor, a soundproof room that had been carpeted in dark blue and outfitted with plush seats and a screen that dominated its south wall.

They climbed the stairs to get there about midafternoon, and when Greta was settled in a swivel chair beside Erik, he flipped several switches on the panel in front of him. Abruptly the lights dimmed and all at once Margo Pierre, dressed in glittering mesh, sprang out of the darkness and began to speak from the screen in the sultry, seductive voice that had made her famous.

Involuntarily Greta gasped.

Erik's dark head came around.

"I'm sorry," she whisperd quickly. "I was expecting credits first — or a lead-up scene."

Erik said sharply, "I told you — these are only clips."

"I know, I'm sorry." She clamped her lips together. Margo Pierre! Why had he begun with her? Did he come up here often to sit in the darkness and stare at his former love? Inexplicably a wave of jealousy washed over her.

But within minutes she forgot everything except the emotion-packed words issuing from that beguiling mouth on the screen and the amazing talent of the sensuous actress who made them seem so real. She had recognized at once that the scene must have come from *Seasons of Torment*, but she had never seen it before. When the clip ended, Erik flipped on the light and Greta dabbed at her damp cheeks.

He surveyed her with a bland look. "Tears?" he said in a sardonic tone.

"Who could help but cry over that?"

Greta said unashamedly. "It was wonderful — but why wasn't it included in the public showing of the movie?"

Instead of giving her a direct answer, Erik rewound the film and started the projector again, dimming the lights to a dull glow. But this time he stopped and started the machine at irregular intervals to point out moments of particular skill and beauty and to remark on ways the scene might have deepened the theme of the movie.

Twice more he did this with additional scenes. Then finally he shut off the projector and leaned back to look at Greta, whose eyes were glowing with the emotion his artistry had stirred.

"What is your judgment?" he tapped his even white teeth with the tip of a pen. "Would the movie have been enhanced if these excerpts had been left in?"

Her breathless answer came quickly. "Decidedly."

"My conviction too." Bitterness tightened the sensuous fullness of his lower lip. "But economics prevailed. It would have run too long, the accounting department claimed and upset the budget by forty or fifty thousand dollars."

Greta protested. "But a finer picture would have resulted. Did they think of that?"

"They don't care about that," said Erik sharply. "Twenty-eight million people paid to see this film without those scenes and came away satisfied. You yourself enjoyed it and never sensed that anything was missing. So you see" — his mouth twisted cynically — "the movie was a tremendous financial success. Who cares — except me — that it wasn't an artistic achievement as well?"

"Surely Margo Pierre cares!"

"If she did," Erik said with a cruel smile, "the two million dollars she grossed from it as it is helped to ease her pain."

"I think it's disgusting that an actress of her ability could care so little about quality."

Erik snorted. "You've misjudged her there. She cares a great deal about quality. The quality of her mink stoles, of her Rolls-Royce, of the paintings that cover the walls of her Riviera condominium."

"But not of the pictures she stars in?"

Erik's expression took on a kind of fiery zeal. "Appalling, isn't it?"

"So that's the reason you walked away from it all?" Greta said.

Erik's smoldering eyes answered, and they sat for a minute in silence, each one absorbed in his own thoughts. Finally Greta spoke in a spirited tone.

"I think you made a mistake. I think you should have stayed."

"What?" His chiseled features pulled together in a look of scorn. "And one of feeling more contemptible with each new picture?"

Greta recalled that Margit had told her Erik had come to Gotland to lick his wounds. Now she understood, and felt a surge of anger. "Not to feel contemptible. To fight for the kind of things you know should be happening in films."

"You're talking like a child. You don't have the least idea what's involved."

"That's true. I'm sure. I'm only a third-grade teacher. But *you* know!" In the semidarkness her blue eyes appeared large and luminous. "That world belongs to you. You helped create it and then you walked away from it when you should have stayed and fought to bring it up to your standards."

Erik's stubborn chin jutted forward. "Margit called you a romantic idealist. Now I see what she meant. But it appears to me she understated her case."

"Obviously you don't know," Greta answered hotly, "but you're an idealist too. Unfortunately your vision of greatness isn't important enough for you to do anything about it except complain. You won't risk a thing for it, will you?"

The accusation fell on Erik like a pan of scalding water. "Listen — " He sat forward and took her shoulders roughly in his strong hands. His eyes blazed, and with a shiver of alarm she felt his hard thigh pressing between her knees. "I beat my brains out in Stockholm for nearly ten years trying to put my point across. Do you know what I have to show for it? I'll tell you — *Seas of Torment* and a few dozen more reels of fakey, phony celluloid no better than it is."

Greta had not guessed that beneath his suave, aloof exterior such rage lay dormant. Although she was shaken by it, she lifted her face to meet his defiant gaze.

"You underestimate yourself. You have a great deal more than what you've named."

"Money — " he sneered.

"You're as crass as those pictures of yours you despise so if you think money is all you've gained in ten years of throwing your soul into your work."

Her outrage cracked wide open her normal reserve. Staring at her, Erik forgot his own anger in the fascination of watching a hitherto unsuspected side of her emerge.

"You have prestige — " Greta's argument gained momentum. "You have a loyal following. You have people like me all over the world with their eyes on you, actively involved with you, practically holding their breaths waiting to see what you're going to do next"

"You want to know what I'm going to do next? Let me show you." He came out of his chair and caught hold of her shoulders. Unaware that his anger had left him, Greta wondered if he were going to choke her.

Then he brought her up hard against him, and she felt the solid wall of his chest bearing into her breast.

"I'm going to kiss you, Greta Lindstrom," he said thickly, and brought his mouth down on hers. For a moment she lost control of her senses. The room spun. She clutched the arms that held her captive and jerked her face away. But with a superior strength he brought her close to him again and sought her mouth more urgently.

She gave a muffled cry, but he caught her nape in his powerful grip and, holding her head still, kissed her again. The erotic pressure of his lips pried hers apart and turned on their softness with a deft and passionate assurance that injected her blood with fire. He kissed her deeply. Desire flooded her. Every sense sharpened to the finest point of scintillation.

Still she fought him, struggling to free herself, but succeeding only in awakening other parts of her body to the pressures of his flesh burning into hers.

When finally he let her go, she came

away from him, trembling and with a wide-eyed stare that dominated the white oval of her face.

"Why did you do that?" she demanded breathlessly.

His own breath came in a rasping spurt. "Because I wanted to."

"Think of Margit! You had no right!"

His gaze hardened. "Were you thinking of Margit? You wanted it, too."

"No!"

Swiftly he brought her to him again. "Do you think I haven't felt the current between us?" His lips moved on the velvet curve of her ear. "All week it's been pulling us closer." His breath curled hot on her neck and shivers splintered through the core of her.

In desperation she pressed with all her strength against his chest. She fell back against his chair, and her hand — going out to recapture her balance — landed on the glowing control panel. Instantly the room came alive with light. Once again Margo Pierre's throaty voice sprang from the screen.

Erik flung out his hand and snapped off all but the overhead bulb, which shone harshly down on Greta's golden head.

His thick voice assailed her. "There's no point in pretending, Greta. You wanted my arms around you. You invited me to kiss you."

She saw the dark, inner softness between the parted lips hovering over hers. She heard his erratic breathing, she felt his hand closing over her wrist . . . A jolting sensation leaped inside her and rippled up through her flesh. She did want him to kiss her, more than anything she had ever wanted in her life.

With a cry she twisted free of his grip and made for the stairs. She heard him hoarsely call her name above the pounding of blood in her ears, but she ran on. The grandfather clock on the first-floor landing struck a quarter past the hour as she raced by it, and then she was out in the sunlight, breathing hard, running.

★ ★ ★

Greta did not stop until she came to the patch of woods that separated Erik's farm from the Olssons'. A pain stabbed at her side. Chest heaving, she caught hold of a tree trunk and closed her eyes. At once the face of the grandfather clock leaped out of the darkness behind her eyelids. Five-fifteen, the hands said. Her blood congealed. Had Margit come? Seen them? And gone away again? What had she done to make Erik think she wanted him to kiss her?

How could this awful thing have happened?

Then suddenly she heard someone crashing through the trees. Erik? Coming after her!

But poised for flight, she saw emerging from the thicket on the other side of the road, not Erik, but a man as tall as he with an unruly shock of blond hair tangled across his brow and a scowl that twisted his face.

Greta's memory whirled — and then she recognized him. Karl Korsmann. The irritable young metal sculptor from Margit's shop.

"What are *you* doing here?" he demanded.

Automatically she responded. "I'm on my way home."

"To America?"

The surly question stung her. "Maybe I am — if it's any business of yours." Then her cheeks caught fire. Subconsciously was she thinking that was what she should do? Go home at once and never see Erik again? More disturbed than ever, she started around the man in front of her, but with another caustic comment he stopped her.

"You'll miss your cousins's wedding if you leave before the month is up."

Greta swung around, amazed that the tautness of his tone so closely matched her own tightly strung emotional state. Then she remembered. His future was bound up with Margit's too. With a recklessness borne out of her own inner turmoil, she challenged him.

"Nothing would please you more if Margit called off her wedding, would it?"

He stared at her as if struck by lightning. "Why do you say that?"

Greta was gratified that she had somehow touched a nerve. "You think if there were no wedding you could go on indefinitely supplying your Venetian signora with Margit's pottery."

"Oh — " Visibly relieved, he murmured, "Is that all you know?"

What else was there? Greta wondered. But at the moment, further speculation was beyond her. This strange meeting coming on the heels of her encounter with Erik had all the qualities of a nightmare. There was even unaccounted-for blood drying in a superficial scratch on Korsmann's right arm.

"I've told the truth, haven't I?" she challenged. "You do want Margit to go on working at the shop."

"I want Margit to be happy."

His hollow answer startled her. In it she heard an echo of her own words to Erik, and the scene in the projection room flashed before her again. Her face flooded with color.

"Good-bye," she said abruptly.

"Wait a minute," he called after her.

Swinging around, she braced herself for whatever was coming next. She disliked Karl Korsmann intensely. Yet at the same time an objective portion of her brain noticed as he approached her the graceful ease with which he moved, the finely made hands that swung at his sides. She was aware too, of a peculiar loneliness emanating from him, the kind of isolated feeling she herself was experiencing. Another time she might have been drawn to explore it, but now she felt only impatience. Why was he detaining her when she so desperately needed to find out if Margit had been witness to Erik's kiss?

Korsmann came up beside her. "Do you know about the party?"

The query, so unexpected and so far removed from what she had been thinking, left Greta speechless for an instant.

"The crayfish party," he said curtly. "It's being given tomorrow evening in honor of Margit — " He broke off as an indefinable change swept over his face. The skin above his collar darkened. "For Margit and Erik Lennart," he finished in a mutter.

"Yes, I know about it." Margit had mentioned it earlier. The two of them were to have gone with Erik. But that was impossible now. All future meetings with Erik were impossible. "Why do you ask?"

His brow knitted earnestly. "Will you go with me?"

"What?" She stared at him.

"Go with me," he repeated. "Let me be your escort. Please." Urgency throbbed in his voice. "It's very important." And then with a tardy attempt at gallantry he added, "I shall be honored."

Greta blinked. Obviously he wanted to use her for some undisclosed reason. The though was repugnant, demeaning. And yet — Her tongue passed over her lips. She had a use for Karl Korsmann too.

She fixed her gaze on his waiting face. "If I say yes, will you do something for me in return?"

A guarded look sprang up in his eyes. "What is it?"

"Will you take me sightseeing around the island?" She saw him hesitate. "Margit is so busy," she went on quickly, "but she still believes she must entertain me. I'd like to show her I can look out for myself."

Korsmann hesitated a moment longer. "Where do you want to go?"

"How should I know?" Greta answered

in exasperation. "You're the one who lives here."

A sardonic smile replaced his scowl. "I have made a social proposal, and you — you are striking a bargain, are you not?"

"What if I am?" Greta flared. "I don't believe for a minute you're asking me out because you're attracted to me."

He seemed offended. "Why not? You aren't bad-looking, you know."

"Oh, thanks awfully!"

"You've a charming disposition, too," he added dryly.

"So have you," Greta snapped. "It overwhelmed me the first time we met.

For a moment they stood glaring at each other. Finally Karl said, "Very well. I agree. You will go with me to the party, and I will take you on Thursday to see the ship-form monuments."

Greta swallowed. Erik had promised to do that . . . they had planned a picnic.

"Well?" Karl waited. "Satisfactory?" he said gruffly.

Greta let her breath out slowly. "Satisfactory."

5

THE farmhouse was oddly silent when Greta entered it. Immediately the apprehension that had been building in her as she came through the woods turned to outright panic. Normally at this time of day Hannah would be in the kitchen. Kenneth would be stretched out on the couch with the evening paper. And Margit . . .

Dry-mouthed, Greta halted midway between the kitchen and the dining room. Where was Margit?

Sick with dread, she made herself climb the stairs, but on the top step her legs turned to rubber. Margit's door was closed. The girls had the whole upper floor to themselves. They never shut doors.

Barely able to make herself cross the hall, Greta lifted her hand and knocked. When there was no answer, she turned the knob and went in.

Margit was flung out across the bed,

her face buried in the crook of her arm.

Greta caught her breath, dread turning into a vicious wave of guilt. "Margit — "

The muffled reply was barely audible. "Go away, please."

"I can't go away!" Crossing the room, Greta dropped to her knees at the bedside. "I have to explain."

"I'd rather not hear about it."

Greta clung dizzily to the edge of the bed. "Please don't cry. It isn't as bad as it seems. Truly it isn't. I can explain if you'll let me."

Abruptly Margit sat up. With a weary gesture she shoved her tangled hair back from her forehead and dabbed with her fingertips at her wet cheeks.

"I suppose he was furious," she said with a half-sob.

"Furious?" Greta blinked.

"Erik. When I didn't show up this afternoon, was he terribly upset?" From under swollen eyelids, her eyes searched Greta's blank face. "Never mind — go on and tell me. I'll have to know sooner or later anyway."

Greta licked her lips. She felt weak enough to faint.

"Well, go on," Margit repeated with sullen impatience. "You said it wasn't as bad as it seems. Does that mean that I'm forgiven?"

"Yes — " Greta found her voice at last. "Erik was — He was upset. Naturally he — " She swallowed convulsively. "He wondered where you were."

"I don't think he has any right to expect me to appear on his doorstep every afternoon like a robot. I have too much work to do." Margit's voice rose. "I can't stop in the middle of something just because it's five o'clock. He should be more understanding."

"He wasn't angry," Greta said quickly.

"You said he was upset."

"Worried. That's what I meant to say. And he — " Greta brought her hand tightly together in her lap. "He missed seeing you."

Margit's face suddenly crumpled. "I had such a terrible headache," she said piteously. "I came straight home."

A headache! So that was it. That explained why she was crying. Greta's blood raced. Thank God! Luck had been with her. On this one afternoon out of the five she had spent with Erik, Margit had come straight home!

Suddenly she felt charged with energy. She wanted to sing or shout. She wanted to take Margit's headache as penance — anything in grateful promise to the powers-that-be that what had happened in Erik's projection room would never happen again.

"What can I get for you?" She leaned over Margit. "Water? Aspirin?"

She had been too frightened to notice before, but now she saw how really awful Margit looked. Her beautiful corn-silk hair was a tangled mess. Her lips seemed as swollen as the flesh around her eyes, and there was a long, thin scratch from one wrist halfway to her elbow.

Greta started at it, oddly fascinated, as something formless and vague picked at her memory. "What happened to your arm?"

Margit's gaze flew to the jagged red mark. "Nothing — brambles." She seemed wide awake all at once. Frenzied almost. Her pink tongue came out and wet her lips. "A bramble bush at the shop — you remember."

Though she had no recollection of anything growing at the shop except what was contained in Birgitta's neat flower beds, Greta nodded. "You should put something on that."

"Yes. Later. I will. Sit down, Greta." Margit's gaze jumped nervously around the room. "Let's talk."

Talk was the last thing Greta wanted. Her escape had been too narrow and she was still shaken by it. "I think I should go down and help Hannah with supper."

"Mother won't be back for supper. Nor Father either. They left after lunch for a cattle auction in Vall. I've been alone all afternoon."

Greta turned in surprise. "But you said — "

"After I came home from work, I mean." A tinge of pink came into Margit's cheeks. She said hastily, "Now come and sit down." She made room for her on the bed. "Tell me, what did you and Erik do today?"

"Nothing — " Reluctantly Greta sank down, her pulse quickening again. "Just the same old thing . . . "

111

Margit eyed her critically. "You sound as if Erik bores you."

"No, not at all," Greta stammered. "He's" — she swallowed — "interesting."

Margit's gaze fell away. "You don't think he was to upset with me, then? When you left, did he seem in good spirits?"

"I left in rather a hurry." Greta picked at the fringe of the bedspread, her eyes averted. "It was late." Relief suddenly swept over her as she thought of a way to change the subject. "On the way home I had an odd sort of encounter."

"Oh? With whom?"

"I met Karl Korsmann."

"Karl?" Margit tensed. "Where did you see Karl?"

"In the woods as I was coming through. He — " Greta hesitated. "He asked to take me out — and I accepted.

Margit's eyes widened. "I don't understand." She laid a cold hand on Greta's arm. "You met Karl as you were coming home? Just now? You say he asked you out?"

Alarmed, Greta saw how pale Margit

had grown. "Is your headache coming back?"

Margit ignored her concern. "Tell me about Karl."

Obviously she didn't approve, Greta thought with a flicker of resentment. "He's taking me to the crayfish party, that's all."

With no warning at all Margit burst into tears.

Greta stared at her, too astonished to speak. Then a flurry of questions tumbled from her lips as she gathered her cousin in her arms.

"What is it? What's wrong? Oh, Margit — " Her heart stopped. "Did you go to Erik's after all? Is that why you're crying?"

"I wanted to go there," Margit sobbed. "I know I should have. But don't you see? It's all so complicated, and I don't know what to do, where to turn — except to you. And now I can't even do that!"

"You can! You can tell me anything."

"When I asked you to come here, I thought I could. I thought you could help me."

"All you have to do is tell me how,"

Greta pleaded. "Whatever has upset you so, we can work out together."

"I think it's too late for that," Margit sobbed. "I'd hurt too many people."

"Margit — " Greta took her firmly by the shoulders. "You're making yourself hysterical. Is it bride's nerves again? Is that what's wrong?"

Margit took a long, shuddering breath and wiped her eyes. "I'm all right," she said in a voice that still quavered. But I can't go on without confiding in you, even if you hate me."

"How could I hate you, Margit!"

"Will you promise that no one else will ever know?"

"I'll do whatever you want."

"Then — " Margit's voice caught. "Then I'll start by telling you about Father."

"Kenneth?" Greta's eyes widened in alarm. "He isn't still ill, is he?"

"No. It's nothing like that," Margit assured her with a watery smile. "Thank God he's completely recovered from the spell he suffered in the spring."

"Then what's wrong?"

Margit chewed the corner of her lip.

"He's losing the farm," she said in a whisper.

The farm! Greta stared. If Margit had said that her father harbored some secret resentment toward Erik or that he disliked the idea of his only child marrying a celebrity . . . but the farm! The Olsson farm had never been worked by any other family. For three hundred years it had passed down from father to son — or, as in Margit's case, from father to daughter. Nothing else in the family's history was valued so highly, even by those who had moved to America. And Kenneth was losing it?

Somehow Greta made herself speak calmly. Her role, she realized dimly, was to help Margit, not reveal her own dismay. "Tell me how it happened."

Already Margit seemed relieved. Some of the color came back into her cheeks. She seemed almost eager now to unburden herself.

"A series of bad luck," she said in a stronger voice. "It began several years back. Saltwater seeped into our orchards and killed the trees. The fruit crop we always counted on to tide us over when the grain failed was no longer available. And the grain did fail, the very next season."

"Yes, you wrote me." But now Greta remembered other things and added them together. The many little signs of deterioration she had noticed around the farm — the need for paint, for repair, for extra help to gather the crop. Her heart went out to her unhappy cousin.

Margit went on. "Last winter a disease ran rampant in our milk-cow herd, a record low temperature killed our first spring planting. A loan fell due. At every setback, Father had to dig deeper into his capital."

Greta nodded, unable to disguise her pity. She had grown up in a farming community and knew how quickly trouble could snowball and take a man down into ruin. "And then your father fell ill," she said quietly.

Margit swallowed back fresh tears. "It was mostly from worry. He never spoke of it, but he didn't have to. He couldn't get well, and I knew why."

"But he's well now, you said."

Margit dropped her gaze. "Because he

has a buyer for the farm." She paused. "Erik."

"Erik!"

"He'd made half a dozen offers before, but Father would never sell to him."

It took a moment for Greta to comprehend. Then she burst out. "But that's wonderful, isn't it? It isn't like selling the farm at all. You'll be married to Erik. The property will still be in the Olsson line."

"Yes." A peculiar stillness came over Margit. "That's right. The farm will still belong to us."

"Then I don't understand," said Greta helplessly. "Why are you so unhappy?"

Margit got off the bed and went to the window. "There — you see?" she said in a tight voice. "I knew I could never explain."

"You *are* explaining." On the point of exasperation, Greta went to her. "But you haven't finished. Is it Kenneth who still has you worried? Are you depressed because even though the farm is saved, Kenneth is losing control of it?"

Margit's blank look told her she had missed the mark.

"Then what is it?" The day's tumultuous events had caught up with Greta, and she felt like shaking the limp girl before her. Yet, on the other hand, guilt was still heavy within her, and she wished for a magic wand that would banish the hopeless look spoiling Margit's fresh beauty. "Please tell me."

"It's not a fair arrangement," Margit blurted out suddenly.

"Not fair? To whom?"

Then all at once Greta saw the whole picture. She recalled Karl Korsmann's sardonic smile in the woods and her own uncomfortable feeling that she was being used. If Erik had wanted to buy the farm before and now Kenneth was selling it to him, Margit might feel . . . of course!

Swiftly she faced Margit. "You silly goose! There's not an unfair thing about it."

"You don't understand," Margit protested.

"But I do! As clearly as if it were printed on the wall."

"I haven't told you everything," Margit said fearfully.

"You don't have to. I feel like a dunce

118

not having caught on before when it's all so plain."

Margit stiffened and pulled back. "Do you think it's that plain to Erik too?"

Erik. Greta remembered his arms around her, his mouth on hers . . . But she must never think of that again.

"Erik loves you," she said staunchly. "It would no more occur to him to marry you just to have his way about the farm than" — she searched for something more absurd — "than it would occur to you to marry him in order to save it."

Margit sucked in her breath sharply.

"Your headache again?" Greta's sympathy was genuine. Poor Margit. Her pale eyes semed to swim even now with some unnamed terror. What a blow her pride must have suffered if she had believed all this time that Erik was more interested in a few hundred acres of land than he was in her! No wonder at times she was caustic with him.

"When you relax and try to see this unemotionally," Greta soothed, "you'll see that you've let your imagination run away with you." I should know, she told herself, bitterly recalling the moments she had spent in Erik's arms.

"There's nothing to worry about," she said with forced cheerfulness. "You do see that, don't you?"

"You've made everything very clear," Margit said tonelessly.

Greta smiled encouragingly. "Then don't look so grim." She hated that hopeless look in Margit's eyes. No bride should appear so haunted. "Your fears are phantoms," she said, though her own heart was aching. "In three weeks you'll be Erik's wife — and Kenneth's worries will be over too. Think of those things."

Margit turned her pale eyes on Greta. "It's the perfect arrangement, isn't it?"

★ ★ ★

After their talk, Margit seemed unusually subdued. All Greta's attempts to get her to speak further about her past unhappiness failed, and finally they went down to the kitchen. Greta, who was herself emotionally exhausted, was relieved when Margit said that probably she should call Erik and explain her absence in the afternoon.

"A good idea," Greta agreed. "Why don't you do it now," she urged, "and I'll put supper together. I'm going to turn in early this evening. It's been a tiring day."

Margit made no reply to that, but went silently into the other room where the telephone was. In a few minutes Greta heard her speaking in a low voice, and she made a conscious effort to clatter the silverware and glasses so that there was no opportunity for her to hear what was being said.

It was astonishing, she mused as she sliced the bread, what a different girl Margit seemed at times from the one who had corresponded with her for so many years. The Margit of her letters had always impressed her as lighthearted and carefree, thoughtful and sweet — far more like the cousin who had met her at the Visby dock than she had ever been afterward. And the last week she seemed to have changed even more drastically.

Greta paused thoughtfully, the bread knife hovering in midair. In the last week Margit's moods had gyrated from frenzied energy to listless absentmindedness. Even her looks had undergone a change, her fresh sparkle giving way to a kind of hollow-eyed solemnity. She seemed crafty and secretive, too, traits Greta found intolerable. Of course it was clear now that she *had* been harboring a secret, but Greta felt there was more to it than that.

Now that she had had time to think about her conversation with Margit, it seemed plain that her cousin had spent all or most of the afternoon at the farm. And Karl Korsmann had been there too. She was sure of it, and that would explain his presence in the woods.

Was he pressuring Margit unduly? When Margit turned up with a headache and left work, had he come after her and demanded her return? Greta scowled. His unreasonableness was probably responsible for Margit's headache. Or, she thought with an uneasy sense of melodrama, was she simply imagining everything?

However, when Margit returned to the kitchen, she made an announcement that was in accord with what Greta had been thinking.

"Erik says that I've been working too hard, that I'm making myself sick." Margit sat down at the table and eyed without interest the plate of fresh fruit and sandwiches Greta had placed there. "Tomorrow he insists that I take the day off. We're going to Botvaldvik for swimming and resting at his beach house." Offhandedly she added, "You're included, too, of course."

"Thanks very much," Greta said quickly, "but I'll stay here if you don't mind. I'd like a day off myself, just to loll around the farm." She forced a bright smile. "I want to do a little reading and catch up on my letter writing."

"You're sure?" But Margit's protest was halfhearted and Greta realized that Erik had not invited her.

Which was wise of him, she told herself, though she was achingly aware again of his mouth turning on hers, of the scent of his skin, of his hard body pressed against her. He and Margit needed to be alone.

That was the trouble. Erik and Margit had spent too little time together lately. And now Margit, freed, for perhaps the first time since her engagement, from the uncertainties that had plagued her, could accept Erik's endearments for what they actually were — an expression of his love.

Greta's heart lurched. What did the kisses he gave to me express? she wondered. Though she chattered aimlessly with Margit while they picked at their sandwiches, the question was still with her when later she climbed the stairs to her room.

Erik's kisses meant nothing, she told herself firmly. Nothing except a foolish, impulsive moment of sexual attraction, brought on probably by the sultry performance of Margo Pierre.

Yes, it seemed logical now to assume that Erik had been reminded of other amours as he watched the film clip, and in reaction he had reached out impulsively for whoever was there.

That was the basic problem, she decided after she had slipped on her gown and sat down before the dressing table to brush her hair. She was there.

She had spent too much time cooped up with Erik. But she woud not allow a repetition of what had happened this afternoon. From now on she would rigidly guard against being alone with Erik Lennart. Quivering, she thought of how close to the edge of disaster they had come that afternoon. If Margit had not had a headache . . . Greta sickened as she thought of how tremulously she had approached Margit's bed and of how narrowly her betrayal had escaped detection!

Even more had been at stake than she had dreamed then. Poor Kenneth . . . what a tragedy that he was being forced to sell the farm, even though it would go to his future son-in-law. But how much more terrible it would have been if, in exchange for the five minutes she and Erik had spent in each other's arms, they had brought crashing down what little security the Olssons had left!

Shuddering, Greta crawled into bed and snapped off the light. Moonlight filled up the room, and she lay staring up at the ceiling, letting herself for the first time examine one dark corner of her heart she had not dared approach until now.

Had she really, as Erik accused, invited him to kiss her?

Did some treacherous side of her subconsciously urge him to take her in his arms? In some wanton movement or tone of voice or look had Erik picked up a signal and acted upon it?

The enormity of her questions rolled over her like a smothering fog. It was true that Erik stimulated her. In his presence she felt more alive, more eager for life than she had ever felt before.

It was true that sometimes when he looked at her she felt that penetrating even the most guarded parts of her being, stirring within her yearnings that made her restless and hungry for some unnamed thing that she felt she could not live without.

But she had never, *never* thought of him as having any part in her life except as the fiancé of her cousin.

Never until this afternoon.

With a smothered sob she buried her face in the pillow. For the first time she had faced the fact that her life was irrevocably changed. When she was running away from Erik, when she was talking with Karl Korsmann in the woods, even when she was with Margit, longing with all her heart to be the strength Margit needed, she had felt the imprint of Erik's lips upon hers. The fire he had aroused surged in her veins. He had marked her, she thought desperately. In those few minutes when he had held her, he had branded her as his. What recourse was there for her except to go on carrying that imprint? Hiding it . . . doing her best to forget it . . .

They would never kiss again. She would never feel his body close to hers. Erik belonged to Margit. That was right and good and as it should be.

Nevertheless, tears soaked her pillow and hours passed before she finally fell into a troubled sleep.

★ ★ ★

The crayfish party to which Karl Korsmann took Greta on Wednesday evening was a festive, joyous affair given each August, Greta learned, by Fredrik and Ingeborg Hannery in their neat little Vall home a

127

few miles from the farm. But this year was special. The invitations had gone out in honor of Erik and Margit, and there were appropriate decorations and many playful jokes directed toward the pair who were soon to be married.

To Greta's relief, Margit had come home from her outing with Erik looking refreshed, if not altogether rested, but as she eyed her cousin across Ingeborg's dining-room table, Greta saw how bright Margit's eyes were. Almost fevered, she thought uneasily. But then Margit smiled up at Erik, and the look she gave him made Greta forget everything except the dull ache that crowded her own heart.

At her side, Karl Korsmann, who seemed to have caught the look too, turned away red-faced and said roughly to Greta, "here — let me show you how to do that."

What he referred to was the ritual of breaking the claws off the tiny red crayfish and then sucking the meat from them. The tasty creatures had been boiled with fresh dill and then piled high on platters down the center of the table. On every side could be heard the musical slurping and uproarious laughter of the Gotlanders as they indulged in this annual treat.

There was not enough meat in the claws, Greta discovered, to equal the size of a toothpick, but what there was had a nutty, sweet taste. Coupled with the piquancy of the dill and the schnapps one was supposed to sip between each bite of crayfish, a rare treat resulted.

This was only an appetizer, however. To appease the hunger of her guests, Ingeborg had baked large round loaves of crusty bread, which she served with spicy links of sausage and several kinds of herring. To wash it all down, a powerful beer referred to by Karl as *export* was poured into mugs that the guests raised in repeated toasts to Erik and Margit.

Greta, who could manage to down only a few sips of the ordinary *dragol*, got by largely on pretense, but it was impossible in the midst of so much laughter and exuberance not to share it, and as the evening passed, she relaxed for the first time all day and warmed to the happy faces around her.

Among the guests there was one young couple who drew her glance more often than any other. Both were fair and of about the same height and age. They looked so much alike that Greta might have thought them brother and sister except for the obvious fact that they were deeply in love. On the way home, she questioned Karl about them.

"You must mean Cal and Eva. He's a fisherman," Karl answered in the abrupt way Greta had grown used to at the party. "Eva works on her father's dairy farm."

Are they going to be married?" Greta asked.

Karl came back at her sharply. "They're half-married now."

She thought he was joking, but he went on in a serious tone.

"*Samvetsäktenskap*," he explained. "Half-marriage. Marriage of the conscience."

Still she was puzzled.

Karl parked his Volvo at the gate of Margit's house and turned in the seat to face Greta. In the moonlight she was struck again by how handsome he was when the sneer he generally wore lifted from his strong Nordic features. She had begun to appreciate him at the party.

When he had drunk a few glasses of *export*, his hostility had lifted, and she had enjoyed watching him joke and laugh with the other guests. It was only with Margit and Erik that he had remained cold and aloof, and Greta found that single mindedness distasteful.

It was understandable that he regretted the breakup of the profitable arrangement he and Birgitta and Margit had enjoyed in their shop, but for him to resent Erik and remain angry with Margit seemed to her childish and silly, and she longed to tell him so. But now she stayed quiet, eager to hear his explanation of half-marriage.

"A couple performs the ceremony themselves," he told her in a toneless voice. "Vows are exchanged — and rings. A tree is generally the altar and sometimes the couple carve their names on the trunk."

Greta saw his eyes darken as he spoke again. "A half-marriage is a firm commitment. One that is never taken lightly. It is a serious matter indeed to renege on half-marriage."

Greta was fascinated. "The union is

respected by the community?"

"Always — if it is known."

"Oh, then sometimes the marriage is peformed in secret?"

He nodded.

"But I can't see the point," Greta said. "If a couple decides to marry, why don't they? Why should they be only 'half-married'?"

"Sometimes it is a question of economics," Karl said sternly. "A couple cannot bear to be apart but neither can they afford to set up their own home, and so they stay separate or with their parents for a year or two until they can go out on their own together and be married by a minister. Or sometimes — " His jaw hardened. "Sometimes one or the other changes his mind. He wants to be married and free at the same time."

"That must make for difficulties," Greta murmured.

"It makes for disaster," he said thickly.

A glimmer of light broke in Greta's brain. Had there been someone among the guests whom Karl aspired to marry? Quickly she searched her memory of the single girls who had been at the party, trying to recall if there were one of them Karl had seemed to notice particularly. Perhaps he had asked her out to make that girl jealous.

"Karl," she said, feeling protective and kindly toward him all at once, "it was a nice evening. I enjoyed it very much. The party was fun and you were good company." Impulsively she laid her hand on his arm. "I hope that whatever your reason was for asking me to go with you worked out the way you wanted."

Just then the interior of the Volvo lit up as the headlights of another car turned into the yard. Before she knew what was happening Karl's arms came around her in a viselike embrace and he bent his head to kiss her.

Greta was outraged — as much with herself as with Karl. She had done it again — sent out a false signal, and look what had happened!

She struggled, but Karl held her fast, his lips moving possessively on hers. In the background a car door slammed and then another. Muted voices passed up the walk toward the house, and wave of anguished humiliation engulfed her. Erik

and Margit! Margit would think she was
brazen to be so intimate on a first date,
and Erik — She couldn't bear to think
of Erik's opinion!

"Please — " Bracing herself, she
shoved against Karl's chest. But to her
amazement he released her as abruptly as
if she had flipped a switch. Sliding back
under the wheel, he opened the car door.
When he came around to her side, Greta
said hotly, "I didn't appreciate that."

"Then I beg your pardon," Karl said
in a voice totally lacking emotion. "I was
only responding to your wish that the
evening had turned out well for me."
With a grim twist to his lips, he added,
"It did. Thank you."

6

THE night of the crayfish party Greta went to bed more determined than ever to have nothing to do with Erik Lennart — except when *not* to do so would create a scene. All evening she had dodged his eyes, meeting them only when they could not be avoided and engaging in conversation with him only when Margit or another of the guests would have thought it strange if she had not.

Erik's attitude toward her had been one of courteous aloofness, though once or twice she had discovered him studying her with a bemused expression that made her heart hammer.

She wanted desperately to know what he was thinking, but he gave her no clue, and as the days passed, she worked harder than ever to put out of her mind all thoughts of the moments when he had held her.

However, it became increasingly difficult

to fend off Margit's insistence that she go with Erik to Visby as they had planned earlier.

Her scheme to sightsee with Karl had fallen flat on its face after his presumptuous and poorly timed kiss. She did accompany him to the ancient cremation grave at Gnisvärd, an excursion that, to her surprise, turned out to be instructive and even pleasant, for he showed not the slightest romantic interest in her, but it was not an experience that she wished to repeat elsewhere on the island.

With curious detachment Karl had explained how the boulders shaping the ship forms that marked the ancient graves had been freighted, perhaps as long ago as 2,500 years, from the mainland. He had his own theories of how this had been done, and Greta had listened politely to his dry recital. But she could not help thinking of Erik's magical way of bringing history to life, and all day, despite her resolves, she wished that it were he instead of Karl at her side.

When they were back at the farm at last, she thanked Karl, assuring him with a sardonic smile that he had more than adequately fulfilled his part of the bargain.

They said good-bye then, both of them relieved.

But Margit was guardedly curious when Karl failed to ask Greta out again. "Didn't you enjoy Karl's company?" she said one morning in a tentative voice as they were dressing.

"Yes, I did." Greta made a great show of enthusiasm. "He's so bright. He has so many interesting ideas."

Nothing more was said then, but after a few more days had passed, Margit ventured another query. "Karl kissed you, didn't he?"

Greta blushed furiously. "I think he felt he should for some reason."

"Nonsense." But Margit was not pleased, Greta could see. "You're a beautiful woman. Who could resist you?"

Greta joked. "I think on second thought Karl could resist me." But she felt trapped by Margit's questioning, ashamed, stupid — and when Margit said firmly at the start of a new week, "Erik is taking you to Visby tomorrow," she could think of no defense."

"That isn't necessary," she said lamely, but Margit countered strongly.

"It *is* necessary. I have an appointment with Lily to fit my dress — and so do you. Aren't you even curious to see what you'll be wearing at my wedding?"

"Of course." But Greta felt only relief. "You'll be going to Visby too, then."

Margit shook her head. "I took the day off to go to the beach with Erik. Now I've fallen behind in my work. But fortunately you and I are the same size so there won't be any problem. You can stand in for me when it's time for my fitting."

"Do you mean you want me to try on your wedding dress?" Greta absorbed her shock with an involuntary shudder. "No. No, absolutely not! It would be bad luck."

Margit made a pretense at laughter. "Don't be silly. Bad luck. That's medieval."

Greta cast about for another excuse. "I'm taller than you."

"Lily will know how to handle that."

"Oh, surely you can spare half a day

to try on your own wedding dress" Greta pleaded. She couldn't do it. *She could not do it!*

"You promised to help me," Margit said, her ripe lips drawn up in a pout.

Instantly Greta was apologetic. "I do want to help. I want to do anything I can to make things easier for you, but to try on your wedding dress . . . "

"Good, then it's settled." Margit left no opening for further objections. "If there are any real problems, I can go into Visby a few days before the wedding."

Then with more emotion than Greta had seen her display in days, she threw her arms around Greta's shoulders. "You're a lifesaver, Greta. You can't know what a relief it is for me to have a whole day free with no pressure from Erik. I can relax knowing he isn't prowling about his house like a restless lion waiting for me to get through with my work."

Greta could not imagine Erik prowling about like a restless lion. He was too purposeful and directed for that. On the days she had spent with him he was always busy. Someone was constantly after him — the sheep foreman or the man who tended the ponies. And there were calls, too, from the mainland, and a great deal of business mail to attend to.

But she kept quiet, bracing herself for the time she must spend alone with him.

The next morning she dressed herself in the least seductive outfit in her wardrobe — a neat blue-striped suit of cotton twill — and wound her hair into a prim knot at the back of her head. When Erik arrived, she was waiting in the sitting room with a tourist's guidebook open in her lap and a pair of glasses she wore only to read perched on the end of her nose.

"I see you're ready," he said with a sardonic smile. "Punctual and proper as always."

He was dressed more casually than she in close-fitting checked trousers and an open-throated shirt that showed the dark mat of hair that grew thickly on his chest. "But never mind the guidebook," he told her in a condescending tone. "I think I'm adequately acquainted with Visby for you to leave that behind."

She hadn't intended taking it. She

was using it only as a prop to let him know what she expected of the day, but smarting from his remark, she slipped it down into her bag and gave him the studiedly impersonal look she had practiced in front of her bedroom mirror.

"I'll bring it along anyway — just to make sure we don't miss anything."

"Suit yourself," he retorted and, with a shrug, led the way to the car.

★ ★ ★

The brief glimpse Greta had been allowed of Visby the day her ferry docked had only whetted her curiosity about this intriguing city, and though she did not look forward to the day ahead with Erik, she was pleased when he suggested they begin their tour by climbing up one of the towers jutting from the wall that rimmed the old quarters. The view from there afforded a panoramic sweep of the island's only city, which had changed little, Erik told her, since the days when it had been one of the great trade centers of northern Europe.

She could see the harbor with its warehouses and the endless rows of townhouses edging into the narrow streets. Outside the wall, red-roofed cottages dotted the landscape.

The wall itself made a two-mile arc around the harbor area. It enclosed the old section of Visby and the nearly three thousand inhabitants who lived there. Greta recalled from her days of study with Erik that the wall had been erected, not for the protection of the Gotlanders from sea-roving pirates, as she had first imagined, but to protect the foreign merchants from the ire of the natives who resented losing control over the island's commerce.

There was a whimsy about that fact that appealed to Greta, as did the looming incongruity of the warehouses against the flat terrain.

"When I first saw them, I thought they were skyscrapers," Greta confessed as she and Erik surveyed the six-hundred-year-old structures that had once held the stores of the merchant princes and still stood in remarkably good condition.

"That's a common illusion experienced

by most visitors approaching the island for the first time," Erik answered. "They're very imposing when viewed from a distance."

Like some men, Greta thought, suddenly depressed. Erik — when she remembered the way she had first seen him — had been imposing too, a prince on a roan horse, a far cry from the dark, flesh-and-blood man brooding at her side.

To divert herself, Greta gazed down at the swarms of people rushing along the streets. It was the height of the tourist season, and looking at the crowds below, she could well understand how Gotland had earned the name of Sweden's Playground. Half of Scandinavia appeared to be scurrying from shop to shop.

When they came down from the tower, she questioned Erik about the influx of visitors.

"We get at least two hundred thousand a season," he told her.

Greta marveled. "It seems strange that all these people could be milling about here when it's so peaceful at the farm."

"Tourists aren't much interested in rural life," Erik replied, steering her toward a church down a side street that seemed less crowded. "They come for the sun and the beaches — and, among other things, to see these."

He pointed ahead at the church they were approaching. "There are ninety-two places of worship on the island, most of them still being used. At the height of Visby's influence there were seventeen inside the wall alone."

"Why so many? There must have been three churches for every inhabitant!"

"Every foreign trading group insisted upon being represented by its own denomination. In the sixteen-hundreds when the city was sacked, many of them were burned, but those that are left are in excellent condition." He opened the door of the cathedral in front of them and passed with Greta into the hushed shadows of the great sanctuary.

"This is one of my favorites," Erik said quietly.

Greta could understand why. When her eyes accustomed themselves to the dim, interior, she drank in the beauty of the polished, carved benches, glowing from hundred of years of use. On the altar, silver crosses gleamed, and marble tablets along the walls attested to the courage of many who had died in ages past defending the island from its invaders.

They lingered in the church for a while, admiring its bell tower and other ornamentations, and then Erik suggested that they move on for a more detailed look at the city itself.

In the church Greta had finally been able to relax, but out on the street she became aware again of the strained relationship between herself and Erik. Driving into the city, they had exchanged few words beyond a couple of stiff comments about the roses that still overflowed from every garden and about Erik's plans for the day. Greta had been aware that they were carefully skirting the memory of how their last meeting had ended.

Was he thinking, too, Greta wondered as she swung along the widewalk beside him, of how she had appeared wrapped in Karl Korsmann's arms?

She still burned with humiliation remembering the way Karl had snatched her to him when the car lit up from Erik's headlights — almost as if he had timed his kiss for that exact instant.

With a tug of yearning, Greta cast a sideways glance at Erik's rugged profile. What a different kiss Karl's had been from Erik's! Karl's forcefulness had held none of the fire and spirit of Erik's embrace. It had, on the contrary, been almost mechanical, whereas Erik's ... she swallowed, her throat tight. She had never been kissed like that. And never would be again, she reminded herself sternly.

But in a moment Erik's tanned arm brushed hers as he pointed out the direction they should take, and her resolve withered under the heated response her senses made to his touch. She could only pray that her face did not betray her inner turmoil.

She hated the power he held over her, and she hated, too, the fact that the harder she tried to dismiss the attraction she felt for him, the stronger it grew.

When he had entered the sitting room that morning she had almost melted looking at his lean, hard body outlined by the tight-fitting trouses and soft shirt he wore. She had caught the clean, enticing scent of his skin as she passed him on the way to the car, and once they were seated beside each other, the distance between them both had been charged with a kind of animal magnetism that she was almost powerless to resist. Two more weeks before the wedding! How would she ever beat it?

Suddenly Erik broke into her thoughts. "Here we are."

Startled, Greta looked up to see that he had stopped in front of one of the warehouses that had been converted into a museum.

"The Hall of Old Things," Erik informed her.

Inside, a priceless collection of island memorabilia had been assembled. Viking treasures, fabulous painting, statuary . . . on every side were new wonders. Erik was especially interested in the tapestry work that had once enhanced the island's churches. Some of it, he said, his grandfather had once handled, and Greta soon caught his enthusiasm for the finely crafted work. While they studied the stitchery, she was able for a time to forget the war waging inside her.

However, when they came out again into the sunlight and Erik announced that they would have lunch at his apartment, her guard came up again.

So this was why he had been so distant and aloof all morning! He had saved his big guns for after lunch.

Well, he would find out, she told herself grimly, that she had no intention of repeating what had happened in his projection room. How she would withstand him, she wasn't sure, but she was determined not to be drawn under his spell again no matter what dark and shabby intrigue he had planned.

Climbing beside him up the stairs of one of the old buildings on the harbor's edge, she nursed her forebodings, but when Erik opened the door to his apartment, she saw that a magic had been performed on the ancient structure and that the elegantly decorated apartment that greeted her was as different from the clandestine hideaway she had imagined as the South Pole from the North.

There was not a dark corner in it anywhere. In the hallway a skylight let in the sun and on a wall painted starkly white, dozens of photographs of actors and actresses hung in black frames. Awards lined the opposite wall and also displayed were numerous other testaments to Erik's fame as a director.

There was none of that at the farm, and several times Greta had wondered why. Now she understood. This was one more way Erik had of drawing a fine line of separation between the side of his life he was trying to adopt and the side he claimed he was rejecting.

In the sleek, understated living room, done in white and beige and accented with black furniture and chrome-and-glass tables, a gathering of men and women were electrifying the air with their chatter.

"Friends from Stockholm," Erik murmured when Greta gasped her surprise. When he began the introductions, she was still too flustered to catch all the names, but she did recognize one or two as persons of importance in the film world.

The guests were bursting with questions for Erik. When was he coming back to

Stockholm? Did he know that Margo had signed with Hollywood? What would his next picture be?

Standing by, Greta was filled with reluctant admiration for the assured ease with which Erik fielded their inquiries, adroitly sidestepping the ones he chose not to answer.

The glances he got were another matter.

Uncomfortably she watched as the women fawned over Erik's dark good looks, and she was grateful when, after a few minutes of responding to the polite asides that were directed her way, Erik suggested she might enjoy looking around the apartment before lunch was served.

She took the bedroom first, pausing on the threshold to gape at the white carpet and then the white fur bedspread, the mirrored wall, and an exquisite collection of Indian carvings done in ebony and expertly arranged on glass shelves.

In Erik's study the painting were sophisticated and abstract. The desk, a prototype for the busy executive, was orderly but stacked with correspondence and scripts. In the dining room the walls, covered in blue suede, set off handcrafted molding, and one wall of glass afforded a spectacular view of Visby's narrow harbor abuzz at midday with the arrivals of ferries and passenger ships.

Overwhelmed, Greta sat down amid this opulence to a meal that began with truffled duck-liver pâté garnished with tomato roses and parsley, and that ended with an elaborately decorated ice-cream bombe. In between, a bewildering array of exotic dishes with unpronounceable names were whisked on and off by two black-coated waiters.

Erik was the perfect host, smiling and attentive, but Greta noticed that he stayed slightly aloof so that his guests were not quite comfortable enough to impose for very long after the meal was finished. When after-lunch coffee had been served in the living room, he skilfully let the conversation wane, and by twos and threes the visitors drifted down the narrow staircase to follow their own pursuits, leaving Greta and him alone again.

When the last guest was gone, Greta released a sigh. "Am I to understand that you call that *lunch*?" She dropped into a chair near the grand piano that filled one corner of the living room and stared dazedly at him.

"It's called a celebrity lunch, I believe," said Erik, dryly taking out his pipe.

"When you're staying here, do you eat like that every day?"

He chuckled. "Felix would love it if I did. But I call him to perform his gastronomic wonders only when I'm expecting guests. When I'm alone, generally the maid's mother from downstairs comes up and fixes a mousse or a bouillabaisse or something simple." His mouth curled wryly as he took a seat. "So you see, it's as I said — mostly tinsel and glitter."

In spite of his attempt to minimize the grandeur of his life in Visby, it seemed to Greta that when they had climbed the stairs from the street two hours before, they had climbed onto another planet. The surroundings, the guests — everything was tinged with a dreamlike aura.

She said so to Erik and watched as the mask he had worn during their tour came down again over his chiselled features. "I'm always glad to leave this place and get back to the country."

"Then why do you come at all?" Greta asked, annoyed. He was not convincing. Despite his stern countenance, there was an excitement about him that was absent at the farm. A keyed-up quality that alarmed her with its sensuousness.

He answered sharply. "I come because it's either here or Stockholm, and I prefer here as the lesser of the two evils. Like it or not, I'm still tied by one foot to my role as director. I will be, I suppose" — his lip curled sardonically — "for as long as my films are showing on Minnesota farms."

Color rose in Greta's cheeks. She could not afford to be drawn back into the easy relationship they had enjoyed before he kissed her. She was deathly afraid of that relationship now. Abruptly she stood up.

"I think I'll go for a walk."

He stayed where he was, sprawled

out in a black chair, the hard lines of his thighs visible through the tightly drawn cloth that covered them. "We were walking all morning. Aren't you tired?"

"Yes — but I'm also stuffed." She dragged her eyes away from his and fixed them on a snowflake cut from silver and dangling from the ceiling. "I can't very well go to Lily's for a fitting feeling like a toad."

His gaze moved slowly up her, drawing her unwilling eyes back to his.

"Nothing about you suggests a toad."

He set his dark head to one side and focused disturbingly on her mouth. "You look," he said quietly, "like a third-grade teacher."

Her color came up in her cheeks as she contrasted the picture he had drawn of her to the sleekly sophisticated women who had just gone down the stairs. "Thank you," she said stiffly, "since that's what I am."

He got out of his chair, slowly, languidly, his compelling gaze still boring into her. "I meant that as a compliment."

Her nostrils flared. "I took it that way."

"I don't think you did." He stood over her, and she wondered, while the palms of her hands turned damp, if he could hear the pounding of her heart.

"I think you are comparing yourself to those women who were here," he said with unsettling directness. "I think they made you uncomfortable."

The acuteness of his perception, which she had often admired, angered her now. "If I'd known you were having a party, I might have dressed differently."

"But since you didn't know, you dressed for me alone and put on your schoolteacher garb. Is that it?"

Suddenly she was aware of how still the apartment was. The chef, the waiters, even the maid had evidently gone. Her words edged past a tightness in her throat. "I dressed comfortably."

His dark looks slid over her, but to her relief he moved away. At the piano he struck a few notes and then turned back to her abruptly.

"What are you afraid of, Greta?"

She caught her breath. "I'm not afraid."

"You're not being truthful. You've

been afraid all day — except for a few minutes in the church."

The way he had of seeing through her was maddening! Tensely she watched him come toward her again.

"I'd like to go walking now," she managed to get out before he stopped in front of her.

"In a minute — " His hand came out and cupped her chin. With the edge of his thumb he slowly traced her bottom lip. She imagined she saw herself reflected in his eyes, pale and trembling. She listened to his breathing, steady and measured, while her own seemed to come in spurts and starts that seared her nostrils.

His other hand curled around her elbow and then slid with erotic familiarity toward her wrist. He pulled her to him.

With his mouth inches from hers, she found herself riveted to his gaze, and she waited, quivering like a hare in a trap, for his lips to cover hers.

"Tell me, Greta," he said thickly, "Why have you behaved all day like an icicle?"

Of its own volition the answer jumped

from her lips. "I don't want you to hurt Margit!"

"Is it I you fear will hurt her?" His gaze narrowed. "Or yourself?"

Recoiling from the cruelty of his question, she shook herself free. "I shouldn't have come here today."

"I disagree." Languidly he watched her move away from him. "What would Margit have thought if you hadn't?"

"She would have believed whatever I told her."

"You're wrong there, too. Already she is wondering why you shy away from me."

Greta's heart lurched. "Has she told you that?"

"Several times." His level gaze was unwavering. "You and I were such good friends for a few days. She knew of our plans to go to the beach house, to the Torsburgen cliff. Won't she begin to think something has happened between us?"

"Stop it," Greta cried.

He approached her again, his unflinching gaze cutting through her like a sword. "*Has* something happened, Greta?"

"You know what happened" You kissed me — and you shouldn't have."

"Is that all?" The relentless, raking passage of his eyes settled on the fluttering pulse in her throat. "Then I won't again, unless you ask me to."

She despised the weakness that made her limbs tremble, that turned her mouth to dust and made her heart cry out for his arms. All her frustration came out in her voice.

"I didn't ask you to kiss me the first time!"

His jaw hardened. "Did you ask Karl Korsmann?"

Greta caught her breath.

"Forgive me," he said coldly. "That was not a fair question."

"Nothing you've done today has been fair!"

"Then let me remedy that." He stood very close to her, so close she could smell his skin, the spicy fragrance of his shaving lotion, the sun-dried freshness of his expensive cotton shirt. "I propose a set of ground rules for us."

Greta stared at him. "What?"

He moved still nearer and she heard

the clinking of his belt buckle against a metal button on her jacket.

"You're aware, of course, that there's a chemistry between us," he muttered thickly, "which is troublesome, to say the least. No" — once again he laid tanned fingers on her lips — "don't deny it. From your kiss I know you feel it. I know from the way you ran away."

His gaze moved over the curve of her breasts. "It means nothing, naturally — nothing except that physically we are drawn to each other."

A pain sharper than a knife blade cut into Greta's breathing.

In the same objective tonelessness, he went on, though in his eyes a fire smoldered. "We don't care for each other — not in any way that matters. How could we when I am in love with Margit?" he waited, watching her face. "And you . . . no doubt there is someone at home who is important to you. Or perhaps Karl Korsmann . . . ?"

He left the question hanging, and Greta bit her tongue to hold back her denial. Let him think she cared for Karl!

Anything to stop this inquisition.

The hypnotic softness of his voice filled her ears again. "So I will tell you how we must behave whenever we are together." His gaze slid over her. "For one thing, we must never touch each other."

Slowly his fingers drew a line across the angle of her cheekbones, and a vivid flush turned her flesh from cream to crimson.

"You see what a touch does," he murmured.

Her first instinct was to cry out, to hit him, to run from the room, but he held her spellbound with his eyes. Her every nerve answered his caress, her lips throbbed in longing, and at the core of her a warm unfurling began that no power on earth could have controlled.

His arms slipped around her, and he brought her close, his lips brushing hers.

"Naturally," he muttered hoarsely, "kissing is out. Unless . . . " His mouth moved, a whisper against hers. "Do you want me to kiss you, Greta?"

Powerless to resist, she moaned softly. For a moment longer he held her at bay, barely turning his mouth on hers in a movement as erotic as a match flaming curling on an edge of paper.

Then the blaze caught.

Yielding to the hunger that swept over her, Greta melted into his arms, feasting on the warm, hard strength of his body, pressing against him, lost in an upward spiral of passion that made her forget everything.

But gradually she became aware that he was taking her hands down from his shoulders. Deftly he put her from him, holding her at arm's length, watching with glittering eyes as, stunned, she struggled to regain her breath.

"There — " He shrugged and with a faint smile said, "You see how it is. We don't dare come near each other."

"Those are your ground rules?" Angry tears stood in her eyes while a devastating shame took possession of her. "They are no rules at all!"

"They're all we have," he answered in a voice made of steel. "But perhaps you aren't up to playing by them, he taunted. "Perhaps it will be too difficult for you to go on seeing me and not touch me, not kiss me — "

She cut in harshly. "You arrogant egotist!"

"Ah, that's better." Now his voice was like velvet, his eyes glowing with challenge. "Perhaps I was mistaken. Perhaps you can handle it after all."

"I see through your game," she flung at him. "I know what you're doing."

"Do you?" His white teeth flashed. "then you know how wise I am. We both love Margit. We can't have her thinking there is anything going on between us, can we?" he paused. "Especially when there isn't."

"The best way to accomplish that," she came back at him, livid with rage, "is to have nothing to do with each other."

"While we're alone, you mean. You can't afford to stop seeing me altogether, Greta. Margit will be twice as suspicious then."

"I doubt if she was ever suspicious in the first place."

His tantalizing mouth turned up. "But you can't be sure, can you? You can't ask her, certainly. And if, almost on the eve of the wedding, you fuel the flame . . . "

In that moment Greta hated him. "You're a devil!"

His only response was to glance at his wristwatch. "You'd better go and get your things," he said coolly. "It's time for your fitting."

Greta trembled with fury. End of scene, take five! But she had no recourse. With a sense of overwhelming hopelessness, she stalked past him to fetch her purse.

7

GRETA had never seen anything as beautiful as Margit's wedding dress.

Her own dress of pale-blue chiffon she tried on first, still so angry at Erik and so sick at heart for the fool her emotions had made of her that she scarcely noticed the shimmering loveliness of her reflection.

She could only think of the decision she had made marching along beside Erik on the way over to Lily's. She would play that little game with which he was amusing himself — and win. He thought she could not resist him, but she would — if it killed her.

But she would not, *could not* try on Margit's dress. That was asking too much, with her every nerve end raw.

However, when Lily came back into the fitting room, her arms overflowing with lawn and lace, Greta felt her objections crumble. Who could look at such perfection and not long to see it on oneself?

The dress was made for a princess, from its dainty scooped neckline to the laced-edged scallops of the hem. A row or tiny French buttons ran down the front to the nipped-in waist, and swirls of white lawn made up the skirt.

"You like it?" Lily's bright face was wreathed in smiles.

Greta was speechless.

"Wait until you see it on — "

Greta kept silent as the whispering cloth slid down her body. She watched the skill of Lily's fingers fastening the buttons into their tiny loops. And then there she was in the mirror — tall and slender in filmy, dazzling white.

A bride. Erik's bride. Her eyes filled with tears.

"You are overwhelmed," said Lily, with satisfaction.

Greta nodded, her throat too full to answer.

"A slight tuck here." Expertly Lily pinned in the waist at the sides. "Less fullness perhaps in the bosom." Lily plucked the pins from her mouth and then stood back. "See? It is perfect!"

Greta saw that it was. Except for the hem. The dress would be too long for Margit. Dazedly she reached for her purse, unwilling even for a moment to take her eyes from the image in the mirror. "Here — " She poked a paper toward Lily. "I have the measurements for the length."

Lily waved them away. "In a minute. It is too lovely on you to spoil the effect now." She clasped her hands together. "My dear, when you yourself marry, you must be sure to borrow this dress. Nothing could suit you more perfectly."

Downstairs a bell pealed. Lily came up from where she was kneeling, her eyebrows arched. "You are expecting someone to call for you?"

Greta shook her head. She had sent Erik on his way with a curt assurance that she could find her own path back to the apartment when the fitting was over.

"Then it is the new fabric salesman," Lily said, going toward the door. "Excuse me for a moment while I call down and tell him to come up."

Lily disappeared, but Greta was too

absorbed in looking at herself in the glass to notice.

"When you yourself marry . . . " she whispered, almost swooning from the longing in her.

Her eyes closed and she saw herself in Erik's garden, the filtered sunlight catching the glitter of dew. It was her wedding day — not Margit's. Her arms were full of roses. And Erik, her beloved, stood tall at her side. A yearning so powerful it was physical forced her eyelids up.

A shock ripped through her. In the mirror Erik *was* at her side. Lips parted, eyes aglow with the same feverish desire that was molten within her, he stood looking at her. Greta caught her breath and whirled. He was there in the doorway beyond her, transfixed.

"Dear God, Greta! — his breath came raspingly — "how beautiful you are!"

The hoarse utterance shattered the spell.

"You can't come in here," Greta cried. "You can't see this dress."

But he paid no attention. Crossing to her swiftly, he took her shoulders, and holding her before him as if a puff of wind might break the fragile illusion, he murmured, "Lovely, lovely. Let me look at you forever."

"You mustn't look at me at all." Greta pushed him away frantically. "Get out Please, before Lily comes back. If Margit finds out — Go, please, *hurry*, Erik!"

The door closed behind him half a minute before Lily bustled back into the room. "Where is the silly man? Did you see him?"

Still trembling, Greta shook her head. "It was not the salesman. It was someone at the wrong address."

Lily was horrified. "A man — and he dared to come up here!"

"You called to him," said Greta weakly.

"But I thought he would use the back stairs. Oh, well . . . " Lily's breath exploded from her red lips. "So long as it wasn't the groom, what does it matter?" She pinched Greta's pale cheek. "You gave him a treat he won't soon forget. Ah, you are a vision, my dear. No bride could look lovelier."

Driving back, Greta and Erik rode in silence until they reached Vall, where the road branched off toward the farms.

Then Greta turned and said in a lifeless voice, "You understand, don't you, Erik, how important it is for Margit not to know you've seen her wedding dress?"

He kept his eyes on the road, but his voice throbbed. "You were beautiful in it."

"Don't say that. You must never mention it again."

"You are afraid of how you looked, aren't you? Afraid of what the dress made you think."

"The only thing I'm afraid of is that you might have spoiled Margit's happiness on her wedding day by barging up those stairs so thoughtlessly."

"I came early on purpose." He turned a gaze of frightening penetration on her widened eyes. "Greta" — his hand reached out for hers — "we must talk. You know that, don't you?"

"I have nothing to say to you."

"Your eyes say a great deal that you can't hide."

Her voice caught in her throat. "Then don't look at my eyes!" She took away her hand. "And don't touch me again — ever."

"That isn't what you want."

"It *is* what I want! What about your ground rules?" she flung at him bitterly. "You're not so irresistible as you thought, are you? It isn't I who am reaching out for *you*."

His jawline hardened. "All right, then, we'll play it your way — for a while."

His menacing tone made Greta shiver, and she turned her face back toward the window to hide the tears that sprang into her eyes. 'For a while' would have to mean until after the wedding, and then she would be out of his life forever, on the other side of the ocean.

Her mind churned drunkenly with mixed emotions, but one thing stood out clearly above everything else. She had fallen hopelessly, helplessly in love with Erik Lennart. In two weeks he would be married to her cousin, but nothing would change for her except that she would go back to America minus her heart.

She realized now that her fate had been sealed the first time Erik kissed her. Instinctively she must have known that, and that was why she had been so frightened and run away from him. But no matter how far she went now, she would never escape her love for him. This afternoon when Erik had kissed her, and later when he had looked at her wearing Margit's dress, she had for a few fleeting moments been a whole person, all of her desires and aims directed solidly toward one goal — a lifetime commitment to Erik.

He was right. She dared not think of that again.

She must be insane to have thought of it at all. What had happened to the sensible, practical girl who had stepped off the ferry in Visby only a few weeks before?

But she was not really sensible and practical. Not where her heart was concerned. Tears stung at her eyes. Inwardly she was filled with romantic idealism — the prince on the roan charger, the fairy-tale princess from

Minnesota. Those childish dreams she had held on to — and today, when she had stood before the mirror in Margit's dress with Erik reflected beside her, her dreams had fused, had become for one brief second reality.

But the true reality . . . She swallowed hard. The true reality was there beside her at the wheel of the swiftly moving car. Erik was not in love with her. He was restless, as Hannah had said, bored and annoyed with Margit — and beyond that, he enjoyed manipulating her, as he had done in his apartment, taunting and teasing until he got the response he sought and then pushing her aside.

Thank God — for Margit's sake, anyway — that this was the case. She must never again forget that Margit was the bride, not herself. Margit trusted her, and she must never come so near again to betraying that trust.

A rough question from Erik brought her abruptly back to the present. "What's Korsman doing here?"

Greta saw that they had arrived back at the farm. Karl's Volvo was parked in front of the house, and he and Margit were seated on the steps, earnestly engaged in conversation.

Her heart sank. Has he come for me? But when Erik's car pulled to a stop, Karl got up at once and came through the gate.

He and Erik greeted each other curtly. Karl gave Greta a nod, and then got into his car and drove away.

Margit came down the path to meet them, a nervous smile lifting the corners of her lips, which Greta noted obliquely, were painted far too red. Or did they only seem to be because Margit was so pale?

"Did you have a lovely time?" Margit called out. Then without waiting for an answer she babbled on, "I hope you saw some of the churches, Greta. And Fiskargränd Lane. Erik?" Margit lifted her face for a perfunctory kiss. "Did you show Greta Fiskargränd Lane?"

"I showed her everything," he answered, and with a fierceness that stunned Greta, he took Margit into his arms and kissed her fully on the mouth.

Margit herself seemed stunned. Breathlessly she wriggled from his grasp. "Erik!"

"I missed you," he muttered harshly.

Greta felt her face flame, and she brushed hurriedly past them.

Margit called after her. "Wait, we need to make plans for the evening."

But Erik interrupted. "You and I are having dinner alone at my farm," he said, loud enough for Greta to hear.

"But we can't," Margit objected in a lowered tone. "Mother and father are away for the evening. Greta will be alone."

"I want to be alone," Greta said in a choked voice over her shoulder. "I have letters to write."

"You're sure, Greta?" Margit stood uncertainly in the path.

Without waiting for an answer, Erik pulled her toward the car.

★ ★ ★

From her upstairs window, Greta watched them go. Be glad, she told herself fiercely. But there was not a glad bone in her body. Her head throbbed, and she felt bruised all over as if a truck had run her down. Erik's final rudeness had cut her as nothing else had.

"Erik is in love with Margit," she forced herself to say aloud. "He wants to be alone with her. He *should* be alone with her."

But her other thoughts she could not voice except in the secret recesses of her heart. Flinging herself down on the bed, she wept until her tears had soaked the pillow. Finally with sea gulls screaming in the distance, she fell asleep.

★ ★ ★

Erik called the next morning only a few minutes after Margit had left for her studio. Greta was busy with a churn in the kitchen while Hannah was outside gathering eggs, and she could scarcely contain her annoyance when the telephone rang just as the butter was coming.

With one eye on the church she lifted the receiver. The solid timbre of Erik's voice came through the line, and she stiffened with apprehension.

"I can't talk to you now," she said curtly when he made it known it was she and not Margit he sought.

"Then listen", he commanded. "We're going to the beach. I'll call for you in an hour."

"I'm not going anywhere with you."

"Of course you are. We agreed yesterday we don't want to upset Margit."

Greta held on to the phone with an icy hand. "We agreed after that to play this my way."

"That was a mistake. I'll see you in an hour," he said, and hung up.

Greta sizzled while she finished her churning, but the butter came in spite of her anger, a round golden ball so creamy and smooth Hannah could not stop praising it.

"You've done your work for the day," she commanded. "Now go out and see the countryside. You'll be going home before we know it, and you won't have seen a thing what with Margit working all the time, and Kenneth and I working — "

"All the more reason I should be working too," Greta said briskly. She had not forgotten Margit's sad tale of Hannah and Kenneth's struggles with the farm, and her anger at Erik intensified.

He was wealthy and careless and had no idea how much damage his teasing recklessness might cause if Hannah and Kenneth — to say nothing of Margit — found out how frivolously he played with his commitments.

Putting her arms around Hannah, she begged. "Don't send me away unless I'm annoying you."

"You annoy me when I think how you'll be going back to America with nothing to tell your family about what this place is like," Hannah replied.

Greta laughed. "I know Gotland like the back of my hand."

"Only from those books of Erik's and a few jaunts around with him and Karl. Have you been to Gnisvärd?"

"I have?"

"To Torsburgen cliff?" Hannah persisted.

"No, but I couldn't go today. Margit left in the car a little while ago."

"You can take the truck."

Greta hesitated. The formidable fortification formed by the Torsburgen cliff suited her hostile mood exactly. "Won't Kenneth need the truck?"

"Not today," said Hannah. "He's helping our neighbor with haying. Take it. Go along with you. But mind the place when you get there. It's wild. Don't go too far into the woods. It's too easy to get lost, even for an old hand."

8

FOR half an hour Greta bounced along in Kenneth Olsson's ancient truck, taking a strange kind of pleasure in the punishment it dealt her on the rough road. How could she have let her emotions go so out of control yesterday that she had imagined herself in love with Erik Lennart? She deserved to be flogged!

But so did Erik. What colossal nerve he had, to call her up this morning and insist they spend the day together, particularly after he had taken such pains the evening before to put her in her place. Clutching the steering wheel, she fought back the memory of Erik's arms enfolding Margit.

There you go again, she scolded herself sharply. She was forever seesawing back and forth. One minute she despised Erik and the next she was consumed with love for him. No sooner had she made up her mind she cared nothing for him

179

than she was dreaming again of his kiss. Perhaps this was the way people felt when they were losing their minds — or their morals!

Her face burned as she thought of the drastic changes a few weeks had brought in her relationship with Margit. For years they had confided everything in each other, and now half her thoughts were traitorous ones she must hide, even from herself. And Margit was different, too.

Watching through the windshield as the greens and grays of Torsburgen's forest came into view, Greta mulled over Margit's behavior that morning.

Greta had risen shortly after seven, and hearing Margit splashing about in the bathroom, she decided not to trouble her for the hand cream Margit had offered for her use, but to get it herself from the dressing table in the other girl's bedroom. But when she crossed the hall, the first thing she saw was that the bed had not been slept in. Margit's freshly laundered dotted-swiss spread lay as smooth and undisturbed as when she herself had laid it on the bed yesterday. The three pink pillows she had so carefully arranged at its head were still in their places.

Her first thought was that Margit had for some reason sat up all night. Then with the tumult of a tidal wave, she recalled waking up just before dawn with the certainty that someone was stealthily climbing the stairs. Thinking she was dreaming, she drifted back to sleep, but with the smooth white bedspread as witness before her, she realized the truth: Margit had spent the night with Erik.

Shaken, she told herself sternly, Well, what if she had? Within two weeks they would be married. This wasn't the Victorian Age. But still the thought that Margit had been with Erik all night numbed her, and she clung dizzily to the bedpost.

She was still there when Margit came out from her shower. When she saw Greta at her bedside, she said in a high-pitched, defensive voice, "How lazy everyone is this morning! I was up ahead of you all, making up my bed, showering — "

Unable to face her, Greta mumbled something unintelligible and, snatching up the cream, hurried out. She felt sick with shame — for herself, for Margit, and for Erik, too. The man of the world who flaunted every convention, spreading unhappiness like poison.

She had no peace from her terrible thoughts until the vigor required to churn the butter had exercised a calming effect. But Erik had ruined that, too, with his telephone call.

Vowing not to give Erik another minute of her day, she halted the truck at the foot of the southernmost tip of the Torsburgen cliff and got out, slamming the door behind her. The purpose of this outing was to take her mind off the upsetting predicament of her life, and she intended to enjoy herself and her surroundings with a vengeance.

Walking along, she gazed up at the fifty-foot rampart scaling heavenward before her and felt relieved that the ponderous embankment made her own petty problems seem insignificant in comparison to the task of climbing it. Surely it must be one of the wonders of the world, she mused. A thousand years before, or perhaps even as far back as the Bronze Age, toiling Gotlanders had blocked off the natural erosions in the limestone cliff with a solid stone barricade that extended for more than a mile parallel to the coast, but some distance back from it. A perfect defense barrier.

The project had captured her imagination when she and Erik discussed it and now, viewing the work itself, she was truly awed. Whatever military chief had devised it, the labor of his followers was still intact even after these many hundreds of years. It hardly seemed possible, but there the evidence was — and all around it were the woods, fragrant in the morning mist and impenetrable, too, as far as Greta could tell. No wonder Hannah had warned her about them.

Still she felt intrigued by the tangling of juniper boughs with pine and spruce, and drawing closer, she saw through the spotted light murky passages that beckoned with an eerie stillness. Sprinkled at intervals like markers were the white-barked birches she loved and somewhere in those darkly recessed paths the *bysen* lived, the elf whose power it was to hold a trespasser in the forest confines for as long as he chose — even for a lifetime, so the legend said. A little shiver of delight stole over her.

Nonsense, of course, Greta told herself but her love of the romantic, of the mystical and magical, pulled her along the narrow trail nearest her. She would go in only a short way, she promised herself. A little peek was all she wanted, just a moment to savor this bit of Gotland folklore that had given her such pleasure when she read about it.

Greta had not counted, however, on the wild flowers blooming along the forest paths, or the shrill, curious calls of a bright bird that constantly eluded her as it flitted from tree to tree. She was pulled on by the scents of the forest, too, and by the mesmerizing play of light perpetually changing patterns on the needle-covered ground her feet followed.

Gradually it dawned on her that she was lost.

The prickle of panic moved up her spine when she realized she was passing — for the second time — a twisted birch whose branches trailed in a tiny black pool.

She passed it once more, and then,

dry-mouthed, she sat down on a rock. Above her the elusive bird called again, and the thought came to her with icy suddenness that this was the *bysen* — the elf in the form of a fowl drawing her in a narrowing circle into the heart of his kingdom.

Resolutely she shook herself. That could not be. But no matter, she was lost anyway, She fought her fright by trying to recall the ways one rescued oneself from this kind of trap. Moss was one way. But which side of the tree was it said to grow on?

Hansel and Gretel had dropped crumbs, she remembered with a pinprick of terror. But she had failed even to bring a sandwich! Her watch showed that hours had passed since she reached the cliff. Her feet ached and she was thirsty. But there was no real need to worry, she reassured herself. Eventually someone would come looking for her. Kenneth and Hannah. Perhaps their neighbors. But how humiliating! Particularly after Hannah had warned her.

Then all at once there was a sound on the path. The snapping of a twig. Her hopes soared, but she tried to suppress them, not daring even to turn to look. Superstitiously she thought, the bysen would love seeing how desperate I am to be rescued! But then she did turn after all because a voice so familiar . . . so dear . . . so wonderfully close by . . . calling her name.

"Erik!" She bounded up. He was only a few feet away, hands on his narrow hips, staring at her.

Without thinking, she rushed toward him. "How did you find me?"

"Hannah told me you were coming here. I wandered around the woods on the other side for a while and then I saw Kenneth's truck." He pointed in the direction from which he had come.

Greta's mouth fell open. Through the screen of juniper needles, she could see — five or six hundred yards beyond — the rattletrap vehicle that had brought her here. Her face turned crimson.

"I thought I was lost."

"So did I." Erik came toward her. "If you had been," he said dryly, "there is only one way the elf would have let you go."

With him standing so near, Greta found it difficult to breathe. Never had he seemed so masterful, more in command of himself. Beneath his clinging shirt she saw the muscles of his chest, solid and powerful, and the dark hair curling at his open collar. In the wan light of the forest he appeared cast in bronze and so compelling she felt faint.

"What could I have done?" she said weakly.

"Shall I show you?" Putting out his hand, he deftly undid the top button of her shirt.

Greta gasped and clutched at the cloth.

"I'm only showing you how to defend yourself against the elf," he said, amused. "According to legend, one must turn one's clothes inside out."

"And how do I defend myself against you?" she demanded, furious at him for taking such a liberty.

Swiftly his expression changed from amusement to alarming directness. "Do you really want to do that, Greta?"

"Erik, stop it!" She was trembling from head to foot. "I can't take any more."

"Any more of what?" He came closer

and in a smoothing, soothing motion moved his hands down her arms. Catching her fingertips, he laid them against his chest and said quietly, "Is it my touch you can't take more of? My holding you close?"

Wide-eyed, she stared at him. "You dare to say that to me? You dare to go on with this game, completely disregarding the havoc you're wreaking?"

He was unmoved. "Is the havoc in your heart, Greta?"

"I despise you!"

"You love me."

In his eyes she saw the fire of passion rekindled and felt it stirring in her own breast. Beneath her fingers his heart pumped with the same erratic force as her own. "I do not love you, *I do not!*" But her tears spilled over, and tenderly he pulled her to him, bringing her head to rest against his chest, while he ran his fingers gently through her tangled hair and kissed the top of her head.

"Poor little girl," he murmured softly. "You have such a terrible conscience."

"And you have none," she said sobbing.

"Would you have me deny what I feel for you and marry Margit?"

"You told me yesterday what you feel for me. A powerful physical attraction."

"God knows that's true," he muttered hoarsely.

She tore herself from his arms. "If I were really decent — really conscience-bound — I'd tell Margit how unfaithful you are." Her tear-stained cheeks were white. "Marriage to you will be hell for her."

He nodded solemnly. "It will."

"Then why did you ever ask her to marry you?"

"Are you calm enough to listen if I tell you?"

"I won't listen to lies."

"Greta — " The softness left him, and he brought her back to him roughly. "We've wasted too much time already. I haven't the patience, and obviously you haven't the strength to go on parrying, to go on pretending that my marriage to Margit can take place. It can't," he said harshly. "It's a foolishness that must be stopped."

"At this late date you can call your

— You can call Margit's wedding plans foolishness?" Greta's eyes blazed. "You allowed her to involve herself this deeply? To buy a dress, to send out invitations — "

"Those are trivialities." His tone hardened. "They mean nothing compared to the waste of two people's lives." He fixed a penetrating gaze on Greta. "More lives than that, if the truth were known," he corrected. "Come here."

It was an order she found herself unwillingly obeying. He took her back to the rock where she was seated when he came up the path.

"You must listen to me, Greta." He sat down beside her, his face rigidly determined. "Margit is not in love with me."

"Don't you wish that were so," she shot back at him. "How much more comfortable you could be, believing that."

A muscle jumped in his cheek, but it was plain he would not be sidetracked by anger. "Furthermore," he went on, "I have never loved Margit. I am fond of her, yes," he said in quick response to

Greta's gasp of objection. "I admire her. Margit is a lovely young woman, beautiful, creative — "

"'Pure' you once called her!" The words on Greta's lips turned bitter as gall. He had called her that once, too, her heart cried out, but she remembered that her heart was not trustworthy, and her tears started again. "Why are you telling me this?"

"Because it's imperative that you understand. Margit will be the perfect wife for another man — but not for me."

Pain wrenched out Greta's reply. "Is that your great discovery from last night?"

His eyes narrowed. "What do you mean?"

"You spent the night with her. Why didn't you tell her what you've told me? Because you lacked the courage? Or because it's a lie?"

Erik snorted. "I had an hour with Margit and it was taken up with dinner and Margit's nervous chatter. Afterward, as always, her work came first."

His burning gaze fastened itself on

Greta's lips, parted in disbelief. "Is her behavior that of a woman in love? On the eve of her wedding does a woman in love spend every moment she possibly can with her hand in wet clay and her heart God knows where?"

"I know she was with you."

"You're wrong." His tone hardened. "I left her at her studio at eight."

Greta looked away, her confidence badly shaken. Had Margit spent the night at the studio, then? A blaze of shame seared her. She had misjudged Margit. While she had pictured her in Erik's arms, Margit had been working through the night to meet her commitment.

"Greta — " Erik grabbed her shoulders. "Have you listened to anything I've said? What I felt for Margit, I still feel, but it has never been enough to build a marriage on. I know that now." His voice took on a hoarse urgency. "Margit knows it, too."

"You're heartless — and blind," she cried out. "No matter how your imagination has enabled you to rationalize things, Margit cares deeply for you."

"Greta, it's you who are imagining things. Open your eyes. Margit is

192

miserable. You have only to look at her to see that. Every day she's thinner, more distracted — "

"And why wouldn't she be — working like a slave?"

"Most of her work is busyness to cover up," he scoffed. "I made a point of going to the shop when I knew Margit would not be there. Birgitta and Karl have been helping with the firing. Birgitta showed me the Venetian pottery. Except for two or three small pieces, it's finished." He looked directly at her. "It *has* been for almost a week."

His positive air infuriated Greta. "How can *you* know how much work she has left to do? Could Margit tell you how to direct a film?"

His patience was fast running out. "Forget Margit for a moment." He made her face him squarely. "There is too much between you and me that is unsettled for either one of us to deny ourselves the opportunity to explore our feelings."

Her voice trembled as a cavern opened inside her, black and bottomless. "I will not allow you to use me to destroy my cousin."

He flushed darkly. "Don't keep on with that prattle. Everything can be straightened out. Can't you see how much kinder it is for me to make a clean break now than to marry Margit and commit us both to a life of misery?"

"That won't happen. After the wedding you'll see how full and joyous your future will be." She saw it herself with devastating clarity. Margit radiant, Erik adoring, both living happily ever after in their fairy-tale house.

She got to her feet, trembling as violently as if a chill had seized her. Never tell me again that you care for me."

He came up slowly. "Think of what you're saying. Don't be bound up in conscience, in honor, in misdirected loyalties, that you deny your own love."

"I don't love you. Why is that so impossible for you believe? You aren't as attractive to every woman as to those fawning ladies you asked to lunch yesterday. To some women you're not attractive at all."

He looked straight at her. "Would you have me believe you're one of those?"

"I don't care what you believe, but I *am* one of those!"

For what seemed an eternity, his gaze bore into her. Finally he said abruptly, "Then I beg your pardon."

She could not bear to look at him, and turned away, but even with her back to him she could still see the stonelike mask his face had become.

"You must forgive me for misunderstanding your kiss," he said in a brittle voice. "For reading in your eyes messages that were not there, for thinking yesterday when I saw you in your wedding dress — "

"Margit's wedding dress," she choked.

"That you were seeing yourself as a bride."

She held herself rigid, fighting down the tremors that were rampant within her. If she moved, even a fraction, she might go running to him, she might hurry herself into his arms . . .

His voice came again. "Was I wrong on all those counts, Greta?"

She must answer him — and answer him convincingly so that once and for all this would be finished. She turned around slowly, willing herself not to focus on the sensuous parting of his lips or on his rugged brow or on his stubborn chin.

"You were wrong," she said.

Their glances locked. Irrelevantly she thought, Will his sons have eyes like those, glowing and depthless?

His jaw tightened. "In that case, goodbye."

He walked away so quickly she had no time to think or cry out. She could only stand and stare after him and then listen as the Porsche's motor sprang to life in the distance.

Afterward, the forest was still except for the call of the curious bright bird that was everywhere and nowhere. Greta sat back down on the rock.

The elf had captured her after all, she thought numbly. In a little while she would make herself get up, move, go forth from this place. But she knew that the part of her that was truly Greta Lindstrom would remain behind, lost among the pines and junipers of the Torsburgen cliff forever.

9

FOR a few days after parting from Erik in the forest, Greta did not see him. Neither did Margit.

He had been called away, Margit explained. To smooth out friction between a film company in Helsinki and his own corporation in Stockholm.

"He says he cares nothing for the film world," Margit said nervously on the second night of his absence, "but plainly he does. There are other people in his office who could have handled this."

"You don't know that," her father remonstrated quietly, but Greta saw the worried look he exchanged with Hannah. Since Erik had left, everyone seemed strained, and as far as Greta herself was concerned, she could hardly swallow past the lump in her throat. The soul-searching she had undergone in the forty-eight hours after Erik walked away from her in the forest had brought her so much pain she was almost sick with it.

What if he really were beginning to care for her as she cared for him? Had she done more damage turning her back on him than would have occured if she had followed her heart and confessed that she loved him?

No matter how hard she tried not to think of that possibility, it continued to haunt her. Every day the awful feeling grew that if there were a villain in this triangle, she was it.

If Erik's plea that they needed time to explore their feelings for each other had been genuine, then didn't he deserve as much consideration as Margit? And what about herself? Though she felt like a viperish traitor, could she go on forever denying her love for Erik? Did loyalty to Margit mean that she must renounce the only man she had ever met who made her feel complete?

Endlessly the arguments plagued her.

Now, trying to appear interested in Hannah's meat pie, which normally she would have found tempting and delicious, she agreed silently with Margit. Erik had gone to Helsinki because he chose to. And not only, she was convinced, because he wanted to punish her and take vengeance on Margit, but because his directing career was still vital to his happiness.

At least in these miserable two days she had come to understand Erik better. It seemed clear now that he had tried hard to immerse himself in the life of the gentleman farmer in order to blot out his disillusionment with his true profession. To some degree he had succeeded. His interest in the crossbreeding of the rams and in perpetuating the *russ* herd on the island had afforded him a great deal of pleasure, but his life's blood flowed only when he was caught up in some aspect of the career he pretended to have rejected.

She had seen the first signs of this when he showed her the film clips. She had noticed then his intense involvement, the undercurrent of excitement that fired his eyes and elevated him to a level of vitality he showed at no other time. Able at last to view with a measure of objectivity that day, Greta saw that the projection room itself was proof enough that he could not relinquish his interest in his former work. If he truly wanted to escape from it, a room bursting with shelves of canned film would never have been included in his retreat.

The day in his Visby apartment had been another instance of Erik's interest in keeping live his connection with films. He claimed he went to Visby only when he could not avoid doing so, but one had to consider that his guests had not come uninvited. Erik did not maintain servants and a chef and those opulent quarters without a better reason than the one he had given her. The truth was, the world of drama was the place where he was most alive, and now, when his personal life was an impasse, he had returned to it to seek to regain his equilibrium. What alarmed Greta most was thinking of the answers he might come up with while he mulled his future in that distant place.

★ ★ ★

Her darkest fears were confirmed when Margit came home early one evening and sought her out where she had gone, feeling desolate and alone, to watch

Erik's wild ponies frolic beyond the fence that separated the two farms.

Rubbing the nose of one of her favorites, a creamy little mare, Greta reflected on the brief time that remained of her visit — and on how differently it had turned out from the way she had imagined. She had expected to go back to Minnesota bursting with the joy of her experiences, but all she felt now was a hollow, restless misery. The bleakness of the future loomed before her, but at least, pray God, Margit would be happy.

However, the moment she saw Margit alight from the Ferrari she knew that something was terribly wrong. For days Margit had been white and silent, but now her face was flaming, and she moved with such agitated swiftness that for a second Greta feared something had happened to Hannah or Kenneth.

Anxiously Greta went forward to meet her. "What is it? What's wrong?"

"Erik — " Margit's voice came out a shrill thread of sound. "He's canceled the wedding."

The ground came up to meet Greta. "He can't have!" She reached out for a fence post. "Oh, he doesn't mean it surely — "

"You should have heard him. You wouldn't say that." Tears spilled over from Margit's feverishly bright eyes. "Greta" — she clutched her cousin's arm — "you must go to him. Talk some sense into him."

"I?" Greta blanched. "Why me?"

"Who else can I send? Father? Mother? How could I do that when this has all been for them?"

"For Hannah and Kenneth? What do you mean?"

But Margit plunged ahead, almost incoherently. "I've been pleading with him myself. He came by the shop. He was like stone, Greta."

"Wait, Margit — " Greta passed a hand over her forehead to clear her thoughs. "You said, 'This has all been for them.' For your parents? What do you mean?"

Margit wet her lips. "I mean — What I'm trying to say — The shock. Yes! The shock will be too much for them. They would never understand what Erik is doing — a week before the wedding!"

Margit seemed on the verge of fainting. "You have to go, Greta. Make him listen to you, even if you have to make promises."

"What sort of promises?"

Her eyes darted about frantically. "Whatever is necessary. You can tell him — " She waved her hands in the air, frightening a pony that had come to nibble at her sleeve. "Tell him if after a fair trial it doesn't work, he can divorce me."

"Margit!"

"Never mind! Don't listen to me." Margit grabbed her shoulders. "I'm crazy, hysterical — "

"Who wouldn't be?" Greta tried to soothe her, but she was racked suddenly by doubts of her own. Was Erik right? Was it true that Margit didn't love him? That she was marrying him for some other reason — money? or prestige? A few weeks ago she would never have thought of such a thing, but now . . .

However, another look at Margit's face reaffirmed her faith in her cousin. Of course she loved him — so desperately she would agree to anything if only he would marry her. Pity swept over Greta, and the last bulwark of her resistance crumbled.

"Shall I go now?"

Margit fell on her with choked sobs. "I knew you wouldn't let me down. Yes! Go now. Hurry! Take my car." But at the last minute her face twisted with uncertainty. "What if he won't listen?"

"He'll listen," Greta promised, but as she climbed into the Ferrari, she was far from certain she could make good her claim. Greta's mouth was dry as dust as she turned up the lane leading to Erik's farmhouse, but within a few minutes her anxiety heightened.

Erik was not there.

The friendly little maid who had so often served them luncheon on the terrace informed her that he had gone to his vacation house at Botvaldvik, fifteen miles distant on the seashore.

"You can easily find it," the girl assured Greta, though Greta was in no way certain she had the courage to look.

"Take the road to Gothem and follow the signs from there," the girl said. "The house is at the end of the main road. It's easily spotted by the weathervane on the roof — a design of Mr. Korsmann's."

Executed when he and Erik were on better terms, apparently, Greta thought grimly as she climbed back into the car. Should she go or not? Perhaps if she waited until morning . . .

But Margit's anguished face rose again before her eyes, and resolutely she turned the car round and headed it toward Gothem.

The miles flew by under the wheels of the sleek, silver Ferrari, Erik's engagement gift to Margit, Greta was reminded. Was it really less than a month ago that Margit with shining eyes had told her that? Less than a month since Erik had stridden up to this same car and fixed his brooding gaze on her face?

How absurd that in so brief a time she had fallen in love with him. But at least when I did, she told herself bitterly, I wasn't on the verge of marrying someone else!

Then a lump crowded her throat. Neither, it seemed, was Erik now.

* * *

When she arrived at last at Botvaldvik, Greta had no difficulty picking out Erik's house from the half-dozen others crouched along the shore. Karl's handsomely made Viking longboat atop the roof pointed into the wind, and striding up from the water with a virile grace came Erik himself, naked to the waist, a white towel swung across his shoulders.

Parking the car, she watched with a hammering heart as he came toward her. If only she were free to run ot him . . . to throw her arms around that broad chest and bury her face in the thick mat of hair that covered it . . .

"Greta?" he came up to the car and stared with surprise through the window. "What are you doing here?"

She climbed stiffly out, wishing, as she watched Erik's plainly admiring gaze slide over her, that she had changed from her shorts into a dress.

He spoke again. "I thought when I saw the car it was Margit."

Unsmiling she said, "I'm here because of Margit."

"Oh, I see." His gaze narrowed. Then

with a sardonic twist to his lips he added, "You should be pleading your own case, not hers."

"I have no case."

He shrugged. "Neither has Margit."

"That's a callous, terrible thing to say. Until an hour or two ago you were engaged to be married to her."

"A sham," he said coolly. "Thank God it's over now." Folding his arms, he let his eyes travel again down her trim tanned thighs. "I should have broken it off long ago."

"Yes, you should have," Greta said icily, "if you didn't intend to marry her. But since obviously you did, to wait until the week before the wedding is unforgivable."

His answering gaze was unflinching. "I'm, not asking to be forgiven."

"Don't you care that Margit is heartbroken?"

He snorted. "Margit is humiliated. I'm sorry for that, but it can't be helped. Besides," he said carelessly, "she'll be smothered in sympathy from her friend, who will have a wonderful time telling her how lucky she is not to have pledged her life to a rake and a scoundrel."

"You're heartless. You can't do this to Margit."

"I have already done it," he answered evenly.

"You've hurt her, yes. Terribly." Greta's voice took on a note of pleading that was completely at odds with the fire flashing from her eyes. "But nothing you've done is irrevocable. You can go to her, patch things up. The wedding can go on as scheduled."

Without warning, he caught her waist and pulled her to him. "The wedding is off," he said firmly. "Canceled. Finished."

With her lips only inches from his she repeated helplessly, "How can you do this to Margit?"

His voice turned to steel, and his grip tightened on her waist. "Did it ever occur to you to wonder what Margit might be doing to me?"

It *had* occurred to her. More often than she dared admit even to herself.

Seeing her gaze falter, he kept his viselike hold on her. "If you had listened to me in the forest instead of affecting noble loyalty, we could have cleared this up then, and with much less pain all around."

"I didn't come her to talk about us."

"Well, we're damned well going to." Taking a firm hold of her hand, he started with her toward the house. "And about Margit, too," he said grimly. "And about everything else that has had anything to do with making our lives such a mess."

In the first room they came to — a sunny, open game room looking out over the water — he pushed her down into a chair and stood over her with menacing authority.

"The first thing I want understood is that, regardless of anything you may think or say, I will not be marrying Margit a week from Tuesday."

Greta returned his gaze, but her blood was racing.

"Two years ago, when I started coming to Gotland," he went on in the same tone of unrelenting assurance, "I met Margit. From the start we liked each other, but a romantic entanglement was the last thing I wanted. The glamour girls — Margo Pierre and her kind — were breathing down my neck. I thought I'd had enough of women forever, but eventually I decided a home and a family were the things that were missing in my life. I asked Margit to marry me."

Greta dropped her gaze, a myriad of feelings clamoring beneath the rise and fall of her breast. How much of this could she take and not give in to those dark, searching eyes that saw clear through to the heart of her?

"I had a great deal to offer Margit," he said with no show of arrogance. "But she turned me down. She was still going out with Karl then."

Greta blinked. "Karl?"

"Korsmann," he said with clipped authority that took no account of Greta's surprise. "But shortly afterward he threw her over. Flounced out of the country and went to Denmark for a month's study. While he was gone, Margit and I became engaged. Oh, I know why she did it," he said without malice. "She was looking for a way to get back at him. But she was fond of me — as I was of her. Our prospects seemed good for a life of contentment together, particularly since neither of us wanted a grand romance."

Greta whispered incredulously, "What *did* you want?"

Erik appeared encouraged by her question. Taking a seat beside her, he reached for her hands, but she kept them tightly folded in her lap.

"I wanted a solid marriage," he answered after a moment, but his eyes stayed on her, burning into hers. "I wanted stability in a wife, the wholesomeness and purity that Margit represented."

Greta stared at him in disbelief. "You knew Margit had agreed to marry you on the rebound from Karl, and you still found her pure and wholesome?"

"I didn't take her affair with Korsmann seriously. Kenneth and Hannah were my friends. I knew the kind of home Margit had grown up in and the values she'd been taught. I thought she would get over Korsmann, and we could be happy. I thought she would make a fine wife."

For all his sophistication and worldliness, Greta thought, he was still as naïve as a child about some things.

"She's no different today than she was then," she murmured. "She will still be a good wife."

"For someone else — as I told you in the forest." This time he took Greta's hands despite her protest and brought them to his lips.

"I know what you're thinking," he said thickly. "What a cold-blooded fellow I am." His eyes moved over her, lingering on the swell of her breasts, on her ripe, trembling lips. "I think perhaps I was that kind of man — until I met you, Greta . . . " he leaned toward her, his voice husky. "My feelings toward Margit are as tasteless as dust when I compare them to the excitement thoughts of you generate." His gaze grew luminous. "You set fire to my blood. All I can think of when I'm near you is taking you in my arms."

Gently he traced the curve of her lips while the thumb of his other hand moved erotically across her palm. "Was there ever any rose petal as delicate as your skin, any sea as blue as your eyes?"

Greta had never wanted him more than

in that minute. Where his hands caressed her, their flesh seemed fused. Her blood sang in her veins, and she thought dizzily, How easy, how simple to slip my arms up around his neck, to bring my lips to his . . . Margit wanted to marry him only to spite Karl . . .

But that wasn't true.

Abruptly she made herself face reality. Margit had never written to her about Karl and had never mentioned him except in connection with her work. If she had ever been in love with him, she would have confided that in her letters.

No — Greta knew it was just as she had first suspected. How long ago that seemed now, that awful moment of discovery when she had realized that Margit assumed a cool detachment concerning Erik because that was his attitude toward her. He had even admitted that just now.

Margit let him think she was paying Karl back by marrying him, but the truth was he was Margit's whole world. Her shaken, desperate cousin who was waiting now for her return might be scarred for life if Erik failed her.

With greater force of will than any she had ever exerted, Greta took her hand away from Erik and fixed on him a look totally devoid of feeling.

"Erik," she said, "you've forgotten what happened at Torsburgen."

He frowned, but still his eyes moved over her with frank desire. "I have forgotten nothing, my darling. I've memorized every line of your body — "

"Exactly," she said coldly. "As you so aptly put it, the attraction is purely physical."

His eyes jumped to hers with a look wary but determined. "Why will you make an issue of that?" he said in a voice faintly edged with annoyance. "Of course I'm attracted to you physically. You're the most desirable woman I've ever known, but that by itself is not nearly enough. There was Margo Pierre," he said in a tone more scornful. "Sexual, sensuous. If I were looking for that alone, I could have had her — and a dozen more just like her."

"You chose Margit."

"Before I met you," he answered

evenly. "Greta, will you at least give us a chance to discover what we feel for each other?"

"What you seem to have forgotten," she made herself say it calmly, deliberately, and with measured conviction, "is that I already know. I am not in love with you."

A dark spot of color flamed at the base of his throat, but he smiled with easy assurance. "I don't believe that."

"Nevertheless, it's true." She got out of her chair, gambling everything on a cool exterior, on this one last thrust. "In a week, whether there is a wedding or not, I'm going back to America. I'll never see you again, and the wife you could have had — Margit, wholesome, stable, lovely — you will have tossed aside on a whim."

Erik came slowly to his feet, his cheeks flushed, but his dark eyes steely. "Prove it," he said quietly.

"What?" She trembled under his penetrating surveillance.

"Prove that you don't love me." His gaze dropped with careful deliberation to her mouth. "Kiss me."

215

"No — " She backed away.

"You never have — not really, not fully." Confidently he advanced on her. "You've fought me each time, struggled, made a big show of resistance. Too big a show, I think."

He stood over her, eyes glittering. "If you don't love me, then what harm can it do for you to kiss me?" He took her face between his palms, the warmth of his hands spreading over her cheeks like a flush.

"Put your lips on mine, Greta," he commanded hoarsely. "Kiss me as you would any man you found attractive — " A smile, ghostlike, touched his mouth. "Let's see what happens."

She trembled. "Don't be ridiculous."

"Don't be a coward." Clamping his hand around her wrists, he drew her, stiff-armed, up against him. "I dare you, Greta. Kiss me."

The chance would never come again. She held herself rigid, but inside, her defenses were crumbling. Already the hard warmth of his body was pressed against hers. Her back arched in protest, but at once his hand was there, sliding

216

under her shirt, smoothing her skin while heat flowed up her spine. His lean thighs hardened, triggering a spasm of desire deep within her.

Just beyond her reach, his lips waited, the full, sensuous bottom lip contrasting sharply with the firm even line of the upper one, tempting her, tantalizing her . . . For one taste of those lips . . .

A moan escaped from her throat. At once his arms closed tightly around her. His head came down, and in a sudden rush of desire she yielded to the urgent demand of his mouth.

Instantly her passion spiraled, flamed, as he took possession of her lips. In a haze of longing she slid her arms up around his shoulders. Ecstasy poured through her as she felt his hands awakening every nerve while they traveled over her body. Inflamed by the potent force of his virility, she pressed against his hard chest; feverishly she kissed the line of his jaw, his stubborn chin, the corners of his mouth.

Groaning, he clasped her tighter, exploring with his own lips the pink shell of her ear, her temples, her eyelids.

The tide of passion crested, they clung to each other.

Finally, trembling, they parted. Erik's hot gaze slid over her, his ragged breathing slowed.

"Now tell me you don't love me," he said thickly.

For a moment she had no voice. She was one single throbbing mass of desire. Only her brain stood apart. Her enemy, her friend. Don't do this to Margit.

With the tip of her tongue she moistened her lips. Swallowing painfully, she brushed a strand of hair from her eyes in a careless gesture. You've proven my point."

His dark brows jumped together.

"Chemistry," she said in a tight voice. "Not love."

He unwound like a steel spring and clutched her shoulders. "Don't lie to me," he said from between clenched teeth. "You are never so alive as you are in my arms."

"I don't love you, Erik."

His hands fell away. His smoldering gaze blistered her with its heat. "You *are* a coward."

"Perhaps." She made her chin come up, though it quivered. "But an honest one."

"Damn you," he said beneath his breath. "You can do this? To yourself, to me?" He caught her roughly once more, his fingers biting into her shoulders. "Don't be a fool, Greta."

"You can't stand to lose, can you?"

He let her go at once and stood back from her, rage blazing in his eyes. "Let's see how *you* like it," he said with savage mockery.

A tremor of fear seized her. "What do you intend to do?"

For a long moment he looked at her, his eyes violating every secret part of her. Then he said in cold defiance, "I'm going to marry Margit."

The knife point of his words stopped her breathing. But that was what she wanted, that was what she had come here for. Desperately she reached for air, pulling it into her lungs, drowning out the hammer of her heart.

"Good," she managed at last, though she was on the point of fainting. "Shall I tell her? Or will you?"

The cruelest of smiles turned up the mouth that minutes before had brought her to the heights of passion. He reached out for her hand.

"We'll go and tell her together."

10

THE week preceding Margit's wedding became for Greta a nightmare.

After her confrontation with Erik, he forced her with robotlike insistence to accompany him back to the farmhouse where Margit was waiting, huddled on a sofa in one corner of the living room. Almost too late, Greta remembered that Kenneth and Hannah must not find out that there had been problems, but fortunately they were off for their evening walk and Margit was alone.

With Erik holding Greta firmly by the wrist, he stood before Margit and said with the consummate ease of the polished performer, "Margit, my dear, I've behaved rashly. Will you reconsider your engagement to me?"

Margit went white. Then flame-red. "Yes — " she gasped, and then burst into tears.

Still Erik held on to Greta's wrist, not

even moving to comfort Margit. When she was in control again, he said calmly, "We owe our reconciliation to Greta. You won't mind if I give her a kiss, will you?"

Before either girl could say a word, he turned and, bending his head, took Greta's mouth with his. From Margit's viewpoint he was apparently bestowing a brotherly embrace, but the kiss was far from that. He forced Greta's lips apart, savagely reawakening her passion.

Blushing furiously, Greta tore herself free.

But still his revenge was unsated. "We must celebrate," he said, making sure Greta could see the adoring look he turned on Margit. "We have a few days left before the wedding. We'll all take a holiday."

"We?" Greta said faintly.

Erik flashed his beguiling smile. "Margit and I — and you and Karl Korsmann."

Greta sucked in her breath and Margit turned white as a sheet, but he went on smoothly, "I've been boorish to Korsmann. An old jealousy," he said, and kissed Margit lovingly. "Now I must make it up to him. We'll have a fine time." His enthusiasm seemed boundless. "We can go to Stånga for the Viking games first and then on to Visby for a few days at my apartment while we do the town. Felix will be beside himself with joy if I bring him four people to cook for."

"I can't possibly go," Margit said firmly.

"Why not?"

"My work."

"Margit, darling." Erik's tone was endearing but rapier sharp. "You've forgotten. Only this afternoon you told me your work is finished. There is nothing you said, to keep us apart any longer."

Seeing Margit's deep flush, Greta mumbled recklessly, "There'll be too many last-minute details to tend to before the wedding — "

"Nonsense," said Erik. "Margit has assured me that everything is ready." He gave Margit a diabolical grin. "If we choose, we can be married today, I am told."

Flinching as he threw back at her the frantic promises she had made earlier,

Margit said hastily, "I'm sure Karl won't be free to go."

"Oh, but I'm sure he will," Erik said firmly. "I'll speak to him in the morning. Or better still. I'll stop by the studio tonight and have a *dragol* with him and persuade him. I want us to be friends again."

★ ★ ★

But they are not friends, no matter what Erik says, Greta thought two evenings afterward, seated in Visby's smartest disco with Karl beside her and Erik across the table, his arm draped possessively about Margit's shoulder.

She sensed their hostility every time their glances met. Still, for some inexplicable reason, Karl had come along on this insane trip and, even more puzzling, had agreed to serve as Erik's best man in the wedding. The friend who was to have performed that duty had been taken suddenly ill, Erik had announced the afternoon they arrived at his apartment.

"Pneumonia, I believe," he said

cheerfully. "You'll be doing me a priceless favor, Korsmann, if you'll stand in for him. And why not?" He slid a jovial smile around the room. "You're a colleague of Margit's, and an old, old friend. It's fitting that you have a part in her wedding."

Karl had looked at Margit then and flushed, but without a moment's hesitation he had answered that he would be honored.

Ever since, Greta had been aware of a curious bond that made the two men allies — but not friends. To her it appeared that Karl was in the throes of some indefinable pain. Since the four of them had been together, he was more affable and agreeable than she had seen him at any time except at the crayfish party, but it seemed hard work for him, and there was an anguish in his eyes that she could hardly bear to look at.

If it were true, as Erik had insisted, that Karl had once been in love with Margit, then perhaps that was the reason. But if he still loved her, why had he accepted Erik's invitation and let himself in for these endless days of torture?

As for her cousin . . . Greta glanced uneasily across at Margit. On the surface she was all smiles and laughter, but at night when they were alone in their bedroom at Erik's apartment, Margit turned limp. Her expression grew haggard and a frightening listnessness took over. More than once Greta had awaken to sounds of muffled sobs.

In the crowded disco the band struck up another raucous arrangement and Karl rose and asked Margit to dance. When they had moved away from the table, Greta turned a stony countenance on Erik.

"You aren't actually enjoying this 'holiday,' are you?"

"Yes. Very much." He lifted his brows and smiled sardonically. Aren't you?"

"You know I'm not! Neither is Margit."

"At least Karl is loving it," Erik said smoothly, and drank from his glass of *dragol*.

"Karl is as miserable as the rest of us," Greta replied. "Please, Erik" — her tone was suddenly beseeching — "can't we go home?"

His eyes glittered with challenge. "Are

you asking to come with me to the farm?"

Her face flamed. "You know I'm not."

As casually as if he were just beginning the conversation, he said, "Did you enjoy the games at Stånga yesterday? The *stångstörtning*, the pole tossing? Or was the *pärk* more to your liking?"

Greta's voice throbbed with emotion. "I might have loved everything. The gaiety, the color, the excitement. I might have loved being your guest here in Visby, pampered and waited on, but you've made it torture for us all, to suit some devilish purpose of your own. I'll never forgive you for that."

In response, an inscrutable look passed over Erik's face, but he only said curtly, "Never is a very long time." Then he stood up to greet Margit as she returned to the table with Karl.

One look at her face, and Greta knew that something had happened on the dance floor. As soon as Erik took her arm, Margit said in a trembling voice, "Can we please go back to the apartment?"

"Is something wrong?" he murmured

with genuine concern.

"Margit is overly tired," Karl said abruptly. "I think she should rest."

To Greta's surprise, Erik let the remark go unchallenged. Tossing a handful of bills onto the table, he put his arm protectively about Margit's shoulders and led her toward the door. As they passed, Greta heard him murmur tenderly, "I've been careless with you, my bride. I've allowed you to exhaust yourself. Tomorrow I think it would be best if we all go home.

★ ★ ★

Over brunch the next morning Margit was edgy and nervous. In the same strained voice with which she had asked Erik to bring her back to the apartment, she informed him that one more chore remain before they could leave Visby.

"Greta and I must pick up our wedding clothes at Lily's."

"I'll tend to that," said Erik carelessly.

"Lily would never allow you to," Margit replied.

For the first time Karl spoke. "It's bad

luck," he said dryly, "for the groom to see the bride's dress before the wedding."

Involuntarily Greta's gaze jumped to Erik. "I'll go," she said hastily. "Margit can stay here and rest."

But Karl, it seemed, had other plans. "Margit is coming with me this afternoon," he announced.

"No, Karl." Margit's sharp response seemed overly positive. "I can't. I'm sorry."

"Oh, but you promised," Karl said evenly. "You would never break a promise, would you?"

"What's all this about?" Erik demanded, looking at Margit's flushed face with a peculiar glitter pinpointing his dark eyes.

Margit answered quickly. "Nothing important."

"On the contrary," said Karl. "It's quite important. The Museum of Contemporary Arts is displaying a joint project Margit and I worked on in May. Last night Margit agreed to go with me today to see it."

An electric silence came over the room. How bold of Karl, thought Greta, asking Margit, symbolically at least, to make a choice between the past and the future. Her gaze went anxiously to Margit's pale face, but it was Erik who spoke first.

"Then, by all means, Margit, you must go." His voice held a keen edge of derision. "Nothing should stand in the way of your and Karl's sharing a moment of appreciation for your last joint creative project."

The three of them stared at each other. Then Karl rose abruptly and, taking Margit by the elbow, steered her from the room. In a few minutes they could be heard descending the stairs together.

As soon as the door shut below, Greta turned to Erik. "What kind of remark was that? It embarrassed Margit. And Karl, too, I think."

"Did it?" He eyed her sharply. "I wonder why?"

"I don't know, but I'm sure you do. And that's why you made it."

He relaxed then, his dark-eyed gaze traveling slowly over her tense shoulders and settling in the open throat of her dress.

The look turned her weak, and she remembered unwillingly that this was the same yellow outfit she had worn when he kissed her the first time. Did he remember too?

But if he did, plainly it was not a memory that stirred him. Pushing back from the table, he said idly, "You worry too much."

"It occurs to me" she said, biting back the surprising surge of disappointment that threatened to overwhelm her, "that you don't worry enough."

Certainly he was not worried about *her*, for all his declarations of caring and passionate kisses! For days his whole attention had been on Margit. He had not tossed so much as a crumb her way, and now that they were alone, he seemed not even to notice. Of course, she would have been furious if he had, but just the same . . .

He interrupted her thoughts with a curt remark. "We're going home today. That should satisfy you. After all, it was your suggestion."

"One you wouldn't have heeded if Margit hadn't been exhausted," she

231

answered with biting sarcasm.

He stared at her for a moment, a curious light coming into his eyes. Then abruptly he turned away and started toward the door.

"Where are you going?" she demanded.

He turned around slowly. "To Lily's."

With a shock Greta realized he was not even asking her to come along. "You needn't bother. Lily won't give you the dresses." She tossed her head to hide her angry tears. "She doesn't even know who you are."

A coldly arrogant smile turned up his lips. "Perhaps she does," he said. "I have sometimes been recognized in surprising places — even halfway around the world in Minnesota sitting rooms."

★ ★ ★

Was there anyone in the world more maddening than Erik Lennart?

Greta stared at his thick neck from the backseat of the Porsche and fumed. Karl was at her side, and in the front seat Erik drove with one arm around Margit.

He had stayed away all afternoon.

232

Half a dozen times she had paced to the windows, picturing him run down in the street by a bus or tripping on Lily's treacherous staircase and tumbling headfirst down it. Once she had even picked up the telephone to call the hospital.

When he finally reappeared at the door of the apartment, he had told her with an annoying little smile. "What a pleasant afternoon. Lily and I had a delightful chat, and then she served me tea. The time got away from us."

"You might at least have called," Greta snapped. "And where are the dresses?"

"Downstairs." He threw aside his jacket and gave her an assured look. We don't want them crowding us on the way back to the farm. Felix can bring them in his car." Glancing around, he said casually, "Margit and Karl not back yet?"

"You don't see them, do you?" she answered acidly.

"Oh, my, my — " Halting before her, he tipped up her chin and said with an amused look, "You've worked yourself up into quite a temper, haven't you?"

Greta blushed and jerked her head

away. "So would you have if you'd had to sit around twiddling your thumbs all afternoon."

Deliberately she chose a chair halfway across the room, daring him with her eyes to come near her. However, he showed no interest in doing so and instead made himself comfortable near the piano, where he picked up a piece of ebony sculpture and hummed a tune while he examined it.

Finally he said, "What day will you be leaving for America?"

Greta's breathing stopped.

Ever since Erik had proposed this ridiculous outing, she had feared this moment. But his earlier snub and the long, lonely afternoon had made it clear that she could not leave Gotland without one more intimate interlude with him. She had the rest of her life to feel guilty about it, but she would never have another day's peace if he did not, just once more, take her in his arms again.

"I'm taking the ferry to Stockholm on Wednesday," she answered guardedly.

"Ah — good." He changed the key

of his tune and whistled the new version through his teeth. "You'll have fine weather for your flight then." Dumbfounded, she watched as he turned the ebony impala between his strong fingers. "I understand the Atlantic forecast is clear for the next five days."

Greta felt as if the ceiling had crashed down on her head. He might at least look at her! The minutes were slipping away . . . they might never have another moment of privacy to say good-bye . . . "Erik — "

But he had taken up a magazine and to all appearance had forgotten she was even in the room.

Shortly afterward Margit and Karl drifted in. The museum tour had done Margit good, Greta saw, but to her dismay she felt only annoyance at her cousin, who for the first time in weeks looked actually blissful.

Karl was jovial, too, and in a few minutes, Greta, the only glum one in the group, climbed with them into Erik's car for the ride home.

Felix, Erik's rotund chef who was coming down to Vall ahead of time to see to the catering of the wedding reception, followed along behind them in his own car, a bright-red Volvo with its backseat piled high with wedding paraphernalia.

In Greta's agitated state, it seemed to her the two vehicles and their occupants formed a regular circus parade. Unaccountably she felt as irritated with the innocent chef beaming from behind the wheel of his car as she felt at Erik.

Margit and Karl vexed her too. Margit had not even asked about the wedding dresses, and both she and Karl seemed as smugly remote in their silence as if they were inhabitants of another world.

Longing desperately for another world herself, she fought back the childish urge to burst into tears and pinned her blurred gaze on the riotously blooming roses that lined the roadway.

11

GRETA woke late on the morning of the wedding with a throbbing headache. All night, elves had pursued her endlessly through a murky forest, taunting her with ribald laughter whenever she begged them to show her the way out. But just before she woke, she had emerged at last into a pleasant clearing where, to her joy, she discovered Erik.

She had not seen him since they returned from Visby until the evening before at a dinner party given for the bridal couple, and in her dream he wore the same light-colored suit he had worn then, his eyes made darker and more probing by the contrast. In the dream he held out his arms to her. Eagerly she strained toward him, but as if mired in molasses, her feet stuck to the forest path and finally he had walked away through the trees, heedless of her cries of help.

Waking up was a relief, despite her

headache, but when she sat up in bed, she saw through the window that rain was falling. In a moment a long-faced Margit came into the room with the same observation.

"It never rains in the summer," she moaned. "It's a bad omen."

"Nonsense." But Greta could hardly hear the sound of her own voice so falsely reassuring. *Rain.* She pictured Erik's garden, which was — in order to avoid the reporters and photographers — to be the setting for the late-afternoon ceremony. She saw sodden heads of roses bowed down with water, soggy paths, drenched guests.

Every detail fit her mood. Her headache worsened, and she longed to close her eyes and not open them again until everything was over. At six o'clock this evening, rain-soaked garden or not, her world would end.

But Margit's would only be beginning. She remembered wearily that she had a lifetime to feel sorry for herself. Today she must think of Margit.

"Don't worry about the rain." She forced a smile and pushed back the covers. "This is only a shower washing the world clean for your wedding day."

If anything, her cheerfulness seemed to further depress Margit. "That day is finally here, isn't it?"

A rush of compassion swept over Greta. The past month had taken a terrible toll on Margit. Her pale beauty had lost its sparkle. She was thinner by at least five pounds and every move she made seemed an effort. Her revival at Visby had been only temporary. Now she seemed physically ill, but Greta was sure that stress was the culprit. She had worked terribly hard for days on end and that, coupled with her uncertainty as to whether Erik would go through with the ceremony, had drained her. Involuntarily Greta shivered. How much more pressure there would have been on her if she had known her cousin had fallen in love with her fiancé!

Turning away, Greta hid the tears that stung at her eyelids. She had not allowed herself to think of Erik since their return from Visby. The hundred times a day he came into her mind, she had made herself remember Margit. She had forced herself to think of Karl, whom she was now convinced was as tortured as herself, and she had thought of Hannah and Kenneth's expectations — any and everything except Erik's lowering face . . . his mouth on hers . . . the warm strength of his body as he held her . . .

Greta clenched her teeth together. Most of all she could not afford to think of those things — particularly today.

Slipping on a soft, striped dress of knitted cotton that clung delicately to her slender form, she ran a comb through her hair and then turned back to Margit, who still sat huddled on the bed staring out at the rain.

"What should we do first?" she inquired of Margit. "Have breakfast?"

Margit shivered. "I couldn't eat a thing."

"I'm not hungry either." Greta pressed her fingertips against her throbbing temples. "Why don't we just go ahead then and get our things together since we'll be dressing at Erik's for the ceremony?"

Margit gave her a vacant stare. "Someone will have to take everything over there later. If the rain stops . . . "

And if it doesn't as well, Greta thought grimly. The wedding would go on, regardless of the weather. The only change would be that the wedding vows would have to be exchanged in Erik's large living room.

Greta thought of the chairs pushed back against the walls . . . of Erik, dark and straight, watching as Margit floated toward him in her white dress. She swallowed back the lump that crowded at her throat.

"Let's start with the dresses, then," she said. "We'll have to box them again, I suppose."

Assuming a briskness she was far from feeling, Greta moved from her closet to Margit's across the hall, carrying the blue gown Lily had made for her draped over one arm.

Trailing listlessly along behind her, Margit said, "I should pack my bag," but she made no move to do so, sitting down instead in a rocking chair by the window and aimlessly twirling a lock of hair around a finger.

"I can hand you things," Greta said.

She brought out two linen dresses and Margit's mauve travel suit. Then she moved farther back into the closet. In a moment she emerged again, holding high a long, airy white chiffon sprigged with tiny blue flowers the color of Margit's pale eyes. The neck was scooped, like a small girl's May-fete gown and the sleeves were puffed and bound on the edges with blue ribbon drawn through narrow eyelets.

"You've never shown me this, Margit. It's lovely.

Glancing up, Margit gave a sharp cry and bounded from her chair. "Don't touch that!"

Greta turned loose of the hanger and the dress slithered to the floor in a wispy heap. "I'm sorry. What did I do?"

"It isn't you." Blindly Margit snatched the dress up again and pressed it to her lips. A torrent of tears began to fall. "I've done something so unforgivable, so monstrous. And now I can't go forward, and I can't go backward either."

Greta stared. Then this wasn't merely another case of bride's nerves? Being careful not to touch the filmy dress again, she led Margit toward the bed. "Here — sit down, she said in the calmest voice she could muster. "Tell me how I can help you."

Margit went on sobbing. "No one can help. It's gone beyond that."

"Maybe if I called Hannah — "

"No! Mother must never find out, nor Father either."

"Find out what? Margit" — Greta dropped to her knees beside the bed — "you can't go on this way. At least share with me whatever it is."

"You'll despise me if I do. I can't bear for you to know how despicably I've behaved."

Now that the initial outburst had passed, Greta found it difficult to take Margit's mood seriously. They had been through similar scenes before . . . Margit weeping and confessing. Margit had more than a little of the actress in her, Greta decided, mopping at her tears with a corner of the bedspread.

"Nothing you could ever do would make me hate you. You know that. Now, please, unburden yourself, or else this afternoon — "

"Go ahead! Say it!" Margit stared starkly at her. "This afternoon when I marry Erik. Oh, Greta! — she swallowed convulsively as the tears began to flow again — "I can't marry Erik." Her voice cracked. "I'm already married. To Karl."

Everything stopped for Greta — the rain on the windowpane . . . the ticking of the clock. "What?" She scrambled up from the floor. "You're *married*?"

"Half-married." Margit took a gulping breath. "Do you know what that means?"

Greta nodded dumbly. She heard Karl's voice again in the dark interior of the Volvo. "A firm commitment," she said without even realizing she had spoken.

Margit's voice caught in a sob. "We exchanged vows in the Torsburgen forest late in March. We meant to be married properly as soon as we could afford to. Then Father got sick. We couldn't wait."

Lifting a sleeve of the film chiffon, she began to weep again. "This was my wedding dress. That's why it had to be you who tried on Lily's dress. If I'd put it on a minute before I had to, I could never have made myself marry Erik."

Shock — the blind anger knifed through Greta. Why *are* you marrying him?"

"You see?" Margit wailed into a pillow. "You do hate me!"

"I'm trying to understand."

"Then instead of jumping to conclusions, why didn't you listen the afternoon I tried to tell you?"

Greta's mouth fell open. "When?"

"The afternoon I stayed away from Erik's farm. The afternoon Karl and I — " Margit whitened, but the outpouring of words went on. "I didn't go to Erik's because Karl and I — We needed each other. We'd been apart so long. Mother and Father were gone. He came home with me. But then I thought I should have been loyal to Erik — I ran away from him, all through the brambles in the woods."

Through the maze of Margit's breathless recital, Greta remembered Karl's strange behavior . . . scratched arms . . . Margit's exhaustion and tear-swollen eyes. This was what Margit had been trying to tell her then? No, it was impossible.

Margit's voice cut through the pain exploding inside Greta's head. "Afterward I realized it was Karl I owed my loyalty to." Her chin came up defiantly. "I've been with him twice since then. At his apartment and in Visby." The hard note in her voice suddenly gave way to a pleading whisper. "He's my husband, Greta."

Agonized, Greta cried out, "Then why in heaven's name are you marrying Erik?"

"Because of father! I couldn't bear to see him lose the farm. I told you that."

Greta was white-faced. "You did not! Not in that way. You told me you were worried that Erik might have proposed to you just to get the farm."

"I never said that. That was your idea. You dreamed it up yourself."

"If it wasn't so, you should have told me. Why didn't you?"

"Listen to us — " Margit's voice broke. "Look at what's happening between us, and you'll know why I didn't" With a sob she caught hold of Greta's shoulders.

"Don't think I haven't seen the

disappointment in your eyes these past few weeks. You've hardly believed that I am your Margit, your cousin, your sister — and I can't blame you. I haven't known myself. I've been selfish, cruel, conniving. But I've been half out of my mind trying to please everyone and pleasing no one. What would knowing the truth have done to you, Greta? Could you have spent one more hour with me if you'd known the real reason I was marrying Erik?"

Suddenly years of loving Margit took precedence over everything else, and with a sob of her own, Greta wrapped her arms about her cousin.

"You meant well. Your heart was in the right place. But it's all such a dreadful mess."

"I'm the mess," Margit said woefully. "All I ever wanted when I broke off with Karl was to help Father." She gulped back her tears. "I was sure I could do anything that was necessary, but now I don't see how I can go through with the wedding. I love father, but in another way I love Karl more."

Numbly Greta realized that since the first hour of her arrival Margit had in a dozen different ways cried out to her for help, but she had been too wrapped up in her own guilty yearning for Erik to see what Margit was trying to tell her.

"I failed you," she whispered through a tight throat.

"Don't blame yourself for anything," Margit pleaded. "No matter what I said a while ago, I'm responsible for everything. And if you hadn't been here, I would have fallen apart long ago."

"That would have been better, wouldn't it? Everything would have been out in the open then, but now — "

"Now it's too late, isn't it?" Margit's wide eyes brimmed with tears.

Greta stared at her. Was it too late? What about her own role in Margit's deception? Margit had worried that she might hate her. Now Greta dreaded what Margit would think of her!

"Start over," she said, buying time while she sorted out her thoughts. "Tell me about you and Karl."

Margit spread her hands helplessly. "We worked together. We fell in love."

"What about when you made up your

minds to marry? Did you know Erik then?"

"Yes," said Margit reluctantly. "He'd even proposed to me once, but I turned him down. I couldn't believe he was serious. He — " A tinge of pink came into her cheeks. "He'd never even kissed me."

Erik had said he wanted no grand romance, Greta remembered, but he had been mistaken about Margit. She already had one.

"Then Karl proposed?" Greta prompted.

Margit's flush deepened. "I proposed to him. I never meant to tell anyone that," she confessed, pressing her palms to her cheeks. "But I loved him so much, and I knew he loved me. He was simply too proud to admit it. He wasn't making much money. I thought he might not for years, and we'd grow old — " She broke off, chewing at her knuckles.

Greta stared at her enviously. If only she were as impulsive and reckless as her cousin! She might have confessed her love to Erik, regardless of the consequences. What would have happened then?

Margit went on. "To boost our income, Karl began making contacts with the continent. Paris, Rome, Venice. The contract that recently came through with Signora Valdetti is one he instigated then. We tried to be prudent, and patient, but our emotions were more than we could handle."

She dropped her gaze. "Shortly after Father fell ill, we married. One day I — " She wet her lips. "I went through Father's private paper without his knowledge. He still doesn't know. I was looking for an insurance policy number we needed at the hospital. Instead I found a document a lawyer had drawn up for Father and Erik."

"The deed to the farm?" said Greta.

"No, not a deed. I don't know what it was — an agreement of some sort — but I saw quick enough what it meant." The color drained from her face. "When Erik proposed again, I accepted."

After a minute Greta spoke quietly. "is that why Karl went away to Denmark?"

Margit blinked her surprise. "How did you know? I never wrote that in a letter."

"You never wrote any of this, Margit. Why not?"

Margit's eyes filled with tears. "With Karl I was so uncertain for a while . . . and then when we married, we vowed to keep it a secret. Karl was too proud to admit he couldn't support a wife, and if I had written to you what I had promised not to tell anyone, I would have betrayed him." Her brimming eyes spilled over. "How much worse I have betrayed him now!"

"Margit, may I ask you something?" Greta took a long breath. "What are your feelings now for Erik?"

"I love him," Margit answered promptly.

Greta felt as if a sledgehammer had fallen on her head.

"But only as a brother — or as a dear friend," Margit went on quickly. "Until we became engaged we had such fun. He and Father were friends, and he came over often. But afterward — " Her voice trailed away into a whisper. "I could never think of myself as his wife. When he took me in his arms, I thought only of Karl."

"I must tell you something," Greta

blurted quickly before she lost her courage. "I love someone in that way too."

Margit's lips parted. "You're in love, Greta? And you've never said a word? Is it another teacher?" she questioned eagerly, her own troubles forgotten for the moment. "Or a farmer near your home?"

"It's neither. Margit, it's — " She took a long, quivering breath. "I'm in love with Erik."

"*Erik!*"

Greta shook her head helplessly. "I know it's incredible, terrible, a far worse betrayal than you've ever been guilty of."

Margit came to her feet. "You're telling me that you've fallen in love with Erik?" she said incredulously.

Greta's face crumpled. "It sounds so plotted put in that way. But that isn't how it happened. Please believe me!"

"Does Erik love you?" Margit demanded.

"There were times when he seemed to." She fought her tears. "But he never actually said so. Now I think he hates me."

Margit's thoughts leaped to another time. "It was because of you he wanted to call off our wedding." She paced to the window and then whirled about. "But I don't understand. It was you who went to him for me, you who persuaded him to come back, to go on with our plans. If you loved him yourself why — "

"He doesn't know I love him."

"Greta!"

"How could I admit that? It was awful enough that I cared for him. How much more awful for all of us if he had known I did."

Margit pulled her up off the bed. "You idiot! You precious, darling idiot," she cried, half in laughter, half in tears. "You must tell him. You must go to him at once — "

"This is your wedding day."

"Good heavens, Greta. I can't marry Erik now — and what's more, I don't have to." Throwing her arms around Greta, she swung with her in a circle. "*You* can marry him! *You* can keep the farm in the Olsson line."

I could, Greta realized dazedly. There was as much Olsson blood in her veins

253

as in Margit's, but Erik ... She remembered the way he had behaved in Visby and his coldness of the evening before, confusing it in her bewilderment with the way he had walked away from her in her dream. "He's never asked me to marry him."

"That doesn't mean he hasn't wanted to — he was already engaged, you know. But now he isn't." Margit jerked off her diamond ring from Erik and thrust it into Greta's hand. "Show him this, then see what he does."

"Margit!" Greta drew back in horror. "You surely don't expect me to break your engagement."

Margit's face fell, and she sank down on the bed like a deflated balloon. "I guess that wouldn't be fair, would it? But there's so little time," she murmured desperately. "And Karl, poor Karl — "

She lifted an anguished gaze. "Can you imagine what he must be going through this morning? And before today, too. Oh, Greta, you have no idea how cruel I've been to him at times. I've almost hated him — even when I loved him the most — because he was powerless to help us.

Because *he* couldn't buy the farm instead of Erik."

All at once she came up off the bed, eyes burning like a zealot's. "I know where I belong. With Karl. And you, Greta" — she snatched up her purse — "you must go to Erik. You must march right in and tell him the wedding is off. And then before he has a chance to breathe, rush into his arms and kiss him. Greta, don't simply stand there and stare. Go put on your shoes — and hurry!"

12

BY the time Greta arrived at Erik's farmhouse, the sun was out in all its glory. The sky was clear and every rose petal in the garden was festooned with diamonds. Feverish activity was occurring there too. An ivory-covered arbor had been set up at one end of the main path, and a dozen workers were scurrying about with baskets of flowers and folding chairs and streamers of gaily colored ribbons.

Tongue-tied with terror, Greta rang the bell.

If only she possessed Margit's free spirit! She might find it possible to rush into Erik's arms if that were the case, but her own reserved nature would never permit that. Particularly now that she had no idea what Erik's attitude was. Did he hate her as she feared? Or was contempt all he felt?

On trembling legs she followed the butler down the wide hall to Erik's study.

He was seated at his desk, but when he heard their steps, he swung quickly around and came halfway out of his chair.

Greta froze, hope hammering at her heart.

But he looked at her for only a moment and then sank back down, the spark of eagerness she had imagined in his eyes fading to a dull glare.

"If you've brought the bride's wardrobe," he said in a flat voice, "Hans can show you where to put it."

Greta's throat closed. Helpless, she stood on the threshold until Erik with a gesture of impatience dismissed Hans and then turned on her with a keen look. "Cat got your tongue?" he said sharply.

His rudeness saved her. "You could at least be civil."

"I am not in the mood to be civil, thank you." She flinched under the scathing look he gave her. "The damned rain has caused all kinds of complications in the garden, and the simpletons who are in charge out there have fallen apart like cream puffs. They've had me up since before daylight with their hysterics."

Nervously Greta parroted Margit. "It never rains in Gotland in the summer."

His lips curled. "I hardly need a Minnesota schoolmarm to give me a geography lesson about my own country."

He didn't need a Minnesota schoolmarm for any other reason either, Greta thought, wanting to weep, but she held on to what little was left of her pride and tried to concentrate on the awful announcement that was hers to make.

"May I sit down?"

He shrugged. "If you plan to stay," he said, and turned toward the window.

Obviously he despised her. Every look he gave her said more clearly than the one before that whatever he once might have felt for her, she had effectively destroyed it. Even in Visby he had not been so hateful.

What if she dissolved in tears? she wondered. What if she wept all over his leather couch? Would he call her a hysterical simpleton? Or would he simply throw her out?

Summoning all the courage she could muster, she said weakly, "I've come to tell you something."

He whirled around, his gaze intense.

"When I'm finished, I'll leave," she said, withering under it.

Once again the glow in his eyes seemed to turn to ashes. "Then be quick about it, please. I've a hundred things to tend to."

Suddenly Greta had all she could take of groveling. "If you'll be quiet and listen to for a minute, perhaps I can save you fifty of them."

"What is that supposed to mean?" he demanded.

"It means — " She cleared her throat. Why wasn't Margit here telling him this? What business of hers was it to be breaking off an engagement that she had no part in? Everything had happened too quickly. What she should have done was to have come afterward with her own story . . . if there'd been any need to tell it . . . which obviously there wasn't . . .

With her heart a stone, she made herself say quietly, "It means that I've discovered something is true that you told me several weeks ago."

He came toward her. "What is that?"

Greta wondered if her face was as red

as it felt. Why did he have to make everything so difficult, staring at her as if his gaze had stripped her naked?

She moistened her lips. "You told me you believed Margit was not in love with you."

He halted. "And you've discovered that she isn't?" He gave her a contemptuous stare. "Is that what all this stammering and foot-shuffling is about?"

"I'm trying to say it tactfully."

"Save yourself the trouble, it isn't news, you know." The flesh above his collar darkened. "But I hardly think this is the time to rake it up again."

"I'm not telling you because it's fun to."

"What is your reason, then?"

Everything came lose inside her at once. She got out of her chair. "Margit has decided not to marry you," she said in a clear flat voice, and dropped the diamond ring on the table.

A long moment of silence followed while Erik's gaze moved from the glittering stone to Greta's white face. Then he said in a voice void of expression, "Why are you telling me this? Why didn't

Margit come to speak for herself?"

"There was someone else she needed to see first."

"More urgently than her bridegroom?" he said sharply.

Greta felt as if he had skewered her onto to a roasting stick and was slowly turning her over a flame. He came a step closer. "Who?"

She wilted back into her chair. "Karl."

"I see." His nostrils flared. "So Margit is finally remembering Karl, is she?"

"If you'll pardon me for saying so," Greta murmured, "she's never forgotten him."

"No?" His scornful gaze swept over her. "She agreed to marry me, didn't she? When I wanted to break our engagement, she sent you rushing over posthaste to patch things up again." His eyes glittered. "What is your explanation for that if she was still in love with Karl?"

"Erik — " Nervously Greta fingered a crystal vase at her elbow and then pulled her hands back into her lap. "In March . . . in the Torsburgen forest, Karl and Margit — "

"Entered into the state of half-marriage,"

he finished for her.

Her eyelids flew up. Erik, hands on his hips, stared down at her. "I've known that since the day I found you lost up there," he said tonelessly. "I suspected it long before, but while I was looking for you, I discovered their initials carved in a wedding tree."

Greta gasped. "You knew and you didn't tell me?"

His jaw hardened. "There were more pressing matters I hoped to discuss with you that day."

"What could be more pressing than that?" she cried, coming to her feet.

"Our own future," he answered in a voice of steel. "Which you summarily dismissed as not worthy of your consideration."

Greta's cheeks turned scarlet. If only he knew! But now was not the time to tell him. That time had passed forever. From the depths of her pain she lashed out at him. "You could have saved us all so much if only you had said something."

His gaze intensified. "Could I have? What could I have done?"

She floundered. "You could have stood

firm when you broke your engagement. You could have set Margit free. But instead you kept her shackled to you out of spite. Spite for me."

"Are you enjoying yourself?" he came back quickly. "Was it only chemistry in your kiss at the beach house?" he said mockingly. "Only physical attraction?"

Without warning he took hold of her shoulders and brought her roughly up against his chest. "You kissed me with your heart, Greta," he said thickly, "but you were too much a coward to admit it. And too stubborn later."

Her heart thundered. "You arranged that trip to Stånga and Visby out of vengeance," she cried, cringing under the painful grip of his fingers. "You did it to deliberately tempt Karl and Margit."

"Wake up, Greta! I told Karl the evening I invited him to come with us that I knew of his half-marriage to Margit. I offered him a chance to do whatever he wanted to win her back — and he took it."

Greta stared at him, openmouthed.

"But even if I had tempted them secretly," he went on in a harsh voice, "they deserved worse than that. I despise the kind of sickly love they share, their on-again-off-again wishy-washiness that lets damaged pride keep them apart."

"Damaged pride," said Greta, recovering her voice. "I'd hardly call Margit's sacrifice that."

"I know of no sacrifice on her part or on Karl's either," he said with brutal insolence. "Unless you want to call Karl's submissive behavior sacrificial. Personally, I call it disgusting. One minute he wants Margit and so desperately he can't wait for a proper wedding, and the next he's willing to step aside and let her marry someone else."

"That isn't the way it was at all."

"You know all about it, do you?" His dark eyes flashed. "It seems to me what little you do know, you've discovered rather tardily."

She twisted free from his grasp and stood apart from him, breathing erratically. "I know one thing that obviously you don't know — though you claim to be so well-informed about Karl and Margit."

"Try me," he challenged.

"Margit agreed to marry you because

she put her love for her father above her own happiness."

Erik scowled. "What does Kenneth have to do with this?"

"Everything. You should have known Margit would find out that Kenneth was having to sell the farm to you, having to let it go out of the family. You were Margit's friend. You should have realized she would never let that happen."

Erik glowered at her. "You're making no sense at all. Kenneth would never sell the farm — not to me or any anyone else."

"Don't think you're going to make me swallow that. Margit saw the agreement you and he had drawn up."

"There has never been but one agreement between Kenneth and me — the loan I set up to help him get back on his feet. But even that he has held off signing until after the wedding so that Margit won't feel her personal decision had anything to do with his."

"You're making this up."

"Ask Kenneth, if you think so," Erik challenged. "In return for the money he needs to get his farm going again, he's agreed to serve as a parttime foreman for my place." Erik eyed her coldly. "An arrangement Kenneth considers quite generous."

"But you wanted his farm," Greta stammered. "Margit told me you've tried to buy it several times."

"I want it, yes. I'd like the increased grazing land for the *russ*, and I'm interested in the crops it produces, but I don't kick a man when he's down. I'd never try to force-buy Kenneth's land. Nor would I ever," he added grimly, "marry his daughter to get it."

"I never thought you would," Greta said hastily.

He snorted. "But you consider it loyal and self-sacrificing of your cousin to marry *me* to keep control of it."

"Margit may have behaved impulsively, stupidly even," Greta replied haughtily. "Perhaps her behavior was even unfair, but her loyalty and her sacrifice can't be questioned." She started past him toward the door. "I think it's small and cruel of you not to at least admit that."

His barbed tone stopped her. "I'm

cruel, am I? I have my own opinion about that."

Taking hold of her arm, he whirled her about to face the garden where the feverish activity she had witnessed earlier was continuing.

"In a few hours," Erik said, "half the population of Gotland will be gathering out there, expecting to witness a wedding. Enough roses have been cut and poked into vases and baskets to fill every house in Visby. In the kitchen there's a seven-tiered wedding cake, a mountain of sandwiches, an ocean of champagne. Whose cruelty is responsible for that may I ask?"

Greta wilted. "Margit has been unfair. I'll admit that. But there's no help for it, Erik." She waved vaguely at the garden. "Trivialities are what you once called such things. You said — " She licked her parched lips. "You said they mean nothing compared to the waste of people's lives." She lifted pleading eyes. "Can't you forgive Margit, Erik? Can't you understand what prompted her to behave so foolishly — and yet so courageously too?"

Erik looked down at her with his piercing, probing dark eyes. "I don't know."

"Can't you at least try?"

"Will you help me?"

Her heart turned over. "What can I do?"

"It's obvious, isn't it?" He lifted his wide shoulders in a shrug. "I need a bride."

Greta sucked in her breath. "You *are* cruel!"

His level gaze held her motionless. "Do you imagine that I'm joking?"

"You certainly can't call that a proposal."

Reaching out, he pulled her to him. "The wedding dress fits you," he said huskily. "Why not wear it?"

Tears of anger and humiliation sprang up in her eyes. "How convenient for you — and how clever! To produce an instant stand-in for Margit. Why not advertise in the newspaper if you're so desperate for a wife? Hire the town crier, engage a skywriter!"

He took her face between his hands. "The position is filled."

"Not by me it isn't!"

She struggled, but he held her fast, placing a tender kiss on the corner of her mouth. She jerked her face away, but he kissed her throat then, and the soft flesh beneath one ear, and her temple.

"Marry me, Greta," he said hoarsely. "I even have the ring."

"Ring!" She gasped. "You'd offer me Margit's? You'd even stoop to that?"

"I'd offer you your own ring — that I've been carrying around for a week. And, yes, I'll stoop too."

Kneeling, he took her hands in his and brought them to his lips. "I never thought I'd say this to any woman, especially one who wouldn't say it to me first." His eyes glowed. "But I love you, Greta. I love you with all my heart and soul."

While Greta stared at him, too overwhelmed to speak, he brought a white box out of his pocket and took from it a diamond the size of a marble, set high in a Tiffany setting.

"I made a good guess," he said with satisfaction, slipping it easily onto her finger. "A half-size smaller than Margit's, even though you're taller." He kissed her lips. "Will you marry me, Greta?" he said again.

Tears trembled on her lashes. "You can't expect me to say yes," she choked.

"I can. I do."

"Until a few minutes ago you were prepared to marry Margit."

"Resigned is a more accurate description then prepared. Even as late as last night I was still confident you'd come to your senses. I was gambling everything on that, right down to the wire. I even spent all one afternoon flattering Lily so she would take the hem out of your wedding dress."

"You can't be serious!"

"Can't I?" he got to his feet, pulling her up with him. "Has Margit tried it on? It will drag the floor behind her."

"How did you dare?" she said, faint with astonishment.

"How could I not?" he murmured. "Weeks ago I put aside all thought of marrying Margit, but openly committing myself to you when you were so adamantly resisting me, went against my grain." Roughly he pulled her into his arms. "You gave me a powerful scare," he said thickly against her cheek. "I did hope again for a minute when you walked in just now, but then I saw you were still as stiff and prim as Queen Victoria, and I thought, Oh, what the hell, what does anything matter anyway, and I gave up altogether."

What if he really had! Greta quivered in the shelter of his embrace. "You don't know how much pride *I* had to swallow to come here."

"You've ample left," he taunted, his lips tracing her cheekbone. "You vixen, you would have walked right out of here, wouldn't you? And never admitted that you love me."

Her voice broke. "How could I? When you acted as though you hated me?"

"I think for a while last night I did." His lips moved on her wet cheeks. "You sat at that dinner table like a graven image."

"Because of you. You were so much the adoring bridegroom, so loving with Margit — "

"The better to push you to the breaking point, my dear," he muttered hoarsely. "Greta — " His voice exploded in exasperation. "Aren't you almost there?"

With a little cry she raised her lips to his.

But he made her wait, touching every part of her face with is eyes, settling at last on her trembling mouth.

Then urgently, hungrily, he bent and kissed her. His hands moved over her skin, tempting and tantalizing her with their touch, molding the curves of her body with a fierce possessive pressure.

Arched against him, she let go all her pent-up emotion. Encircling his nape, she ran her fingers through his dark hair, thrilling as it sprang away with a vigor of its own. Exultantly she felt the rise of his muscles, the virile persuasion of his hardened body, the sheer strength of him straining toward her.

"Oh, my darling." She pressed her face to his. "I love you, I love you — "

Caught up in a relentless tide of passion, they swayed together, arms locking their bodies, every caress signaling renewed stimulation until, inflamed with desire, they forced themselves to pull apart.

Erik's breath came heavily. "Only a

few more hours, my precious one, then you'll be mine."

Greta gazed at him. "Do you actually mean we're to be married today?"

"Can you think of a better time? of course" — his eyes took on a guarded look — "there are certain practicalities — one in particular — that we have to consider first."

He sounded so grim all at once that her heart came up in her throat.

"Where do you want to live?" he said.

She went weak with relief. "Here on the farm," she answered without thinking. "Isn't that what you want?"

"I once thought so."

"Oh, Erik!" Suddenly her heart was bursting with renewed joy. "You're thinking of taking up your career again, aren't you?"

"Will you mind terribly?"

"Mind? Laughter bubbled up from her throat. "I'm the one who nagged you to begin with, remember?"

He nodded and kissed her lips again. "You challenged me," he said thickly. "I couldn't rest afterward until I'd mulled it all over and made a decision."

"I think you made the decision long ago," she said quietly. "As far back as your asking Kenneth to be your parttime foreman."

He brought his arms around her and held her close against his wide chest. "It will be a very different life for you, my love. A difficult one at times, I'm afraid."

"You'll be at my side," she said contentedly.

"Always. I promise that."

"Will we go to Stockholm?" she said, already dreaming.

But he startled her with is answer. "I want to go to America first."

She pulled back, eyes opened wide. "America! Do you mean it?"

"I want to work for a time in California and in New York." He stroked her cheek. "And I want to get to know my Minnesota family."

"Oh, Erik!"

"Afterward we'll come home." he smiled reassuringly. "To Gotland. The farm will always be home, but we'll be spending time in Visby, too, and in Stockholm."

"And in Botvaldvik, I hope," said Greta, remembering with a tightness in her throat how Erik had held her there and how perilously close she had come then to giving herself away. "What about Kenneth and Hannah?" she said suddenly, truly facing for the first time the reality of what Erik was proposing they do in just a few hours. "What about all the guests who are coming here expecting Margit to be the bride this evening?"

Erik kissed her brow. "They'll be surprised, won't they?"

"Erik!" Greta was genuinely troubled. "They'll be shocked. My appearance will cause such a sensation the whole beauty and meaning of the ceremony will be spoiled. And I could never hurt Hannah and Kenneth that way."

"You're right, of course. There are certain steps we have to take, and we haven't much time." Briskly he got up and strode to the telephone. Within minutes he had spoken to Karl and Margit and then to Hannah and Kenneth.

Turning back toward Greta, he said with perfect assurance, "They'll be here

275

shortly. Everything will be taken care of."

Greta came to him and laid her head gratefully on his chest. "After we're married," she said softly, "will you always be able to solve my problems so easily?"

"Always," he promised, and made his kiss the guarantee.

13

AT a quarter to six when the guests began arriving at Erik's farm, the host himself greeted them.

"Make yourselves comfortable in the living room," he told each one. "Kenneth and Hannah are there with champagne, and I'll be along soon myself with an announcement."

When the puzzled but animated group were finally all assembled, Erik appeared with Karl at his side.

"Margit and I," he began when every eye was on him, "are grateful that each of you has come here this evening to join with us in celebration." He glanced at Karl. "But we have a surprise. Instead of the single wedding to which you were invited, I am pleased to tell you that we will be presenting a double bill."

This startling pronouncement, coupled with Erik's film-world terminology, produced the flurry of titters and raised eyebrows that he intended. Then with that out of the way, he skillfully subdued them with a sudden serious tone.

"Karl Korsmann, whom you all know, has honored me by consenting to serve as my best man, and afterward" — Erik paused, his keen glance going around the room — "it will be my privilege to serve as his."

Again the murmurs rose but quickly quieted when Erik began to speak, this time in the resonant, persuasive voice that Greta loved so well.

"We are all friends who have gathered here, and I am sure you would agree with me that each of us is a complex creature with a variety of loyalties and loves. Sometime in the course of our daily lives we find that in being faithful to one, we transgress against another."

He paused again, his level gaze sweeping the silent room. "Such is the case here today. Therefore" — his voice resounded firmly — "Margit Olsson and I will not be married in my garden this evening."

He waited while the audience reacted with gasps of astonishment and bewilderment. Then he went calmly on.

"Instead, Margit will, with my blessing and good wishes, pledge the final vows of her half-marriage to Karl Korsmann.

"As for myself" — he brought up his hand to silence the ensuing hubbub — "it will be my honor and my joy to be joined in holy wedlock with the young woman I cherish above all other human beings — Margit's cousin from America, Greta Lindstrom."

Stepping back a place, he opened the door into the study.

In shimmering loveliness Greta emerged, carrying a mixed bouquet of island flowers and wearing the exquisitely detailed gown she had inadvertently modeled for Erik in Lily's apartment in Visby.

But there was no fear on her face of bad omens. Instead, her smile was radiant, and she took Erik's extended hand with poised assurance and a look of love that melted every heart there.

Behind her came Margit, her delicate face aglow with happiness, and her slim form arrayed in the blue-sprigged chiffon she had worn to her first wedding.

The foursome, followed by a jubilant

Kenneth and Hannah and an amazed but inspired assemblage of guests, trailed out into the twilight. Under the ivy-twined arbor the two couples exchanged their vows in a solemn finish to a ceremony unprecedented in all the island's history.

As soon as it was over, Erik skillfully drew Greta back into the study.

"But our guests," she laughingly protested when he had closed the door and wrapped his arms around her. What about our guests?"

"Let them eat cake," he answered hoarsely, "while you kiss me, Mrs. Lennart."

TO FIGHT THE WILD
Rod Ansell and Rachel Percy

Lost in uncharted Australian bush, Rod Ansell survived by hunting and trapping wild animals, improvising shelter and using all the bushman's skills he knew.

COROMANDEL
Pat Barr

India in the 1830s is a hot, uncomfortable place, where the East India Company still rules. Amelia and her new husband find themselves caught up in the animosities which seethe between the old order and the new.

THE SMALL PARTY
Lillian Beckwith

A frightening journey to safety begins for Ruth and her small party as their island is caught up in the dangers of armed insurrection.

THE WILDERNESS WALK
Sheila Bishop

Stifling unpleasant memories of a misbegotten romance in Cleave with Lord Francis Aubrey, Lavinia goes on holiday there with her sister. The two women are thrust into a romantic intrigue involving none other than Lord Francis.

THE RELUCTANT GUEST
Rosalind Brett

Ann Calvert went to spend a month on a South African farm with Theo Borland and his sister. They both proved to be different from her first idea of them, and there was Storr Peterson — the most disturbing man she had ever met.

ONE ENCHANTED SUMMER
Anne Tedlock Brooks

A tale of mystery and romance and a girl who found both during one enchanted summer.